Artful Deception

Artful Deception

a novel

Peggy Spear

to Jody, Rene, and Abby,
with love!
Peggy

Deeds Publishing | Atlanta

Published by Deeds Publishing in Athens, GA
www.deedspublishing.com

Printed in The United States of America

Text Layout and cover design by Mark Babcock

Library of Congress Cataloging-in-Publications data is available upon request.

ISBN 978-1-944193-90-4
EISBN 978-1-944193-91-1

Books are available in quantity for promotional or premium use. For information, email info@deedspublishing.com.

First Edition, 2017

1 2 3 4 5 6 7 8 9 0

For Eric Duggan, Jr.
1955 - 2015

1. SATURDAY

Out of nowhere, an image arose in the old man's mind: dozens of bottle caps half-buried in the hard dirt... Orange Crush, Nu-Grape, and Strawberry scattered among RC, Pepsi, and Coca-Cola caps, making a wild mosaic on the ground. Boisterous youngsters and weary working men with their sack lunches would walk out of the corner Weona Grocery with their bottles icy cold from the cooler inside and pop the caps on the opener nailed into the brick wall. Bottle caps flew to the ground and, over time, were pressed into the dirt. No one picked them up. There were no litter laws then, there was no sidewalk, and the half-buried caps served a purpose of a sort, a scattering of colorful metal bits that hardened the earthen path for customers and kids on their bikes.

Not like today, Frank thought, eying the manicured grass and debris-free sidewalks in front of the homes and shops he ambled past. In the distance, he could hear the annoying whine of a leaf blower.

He wondered why he thought of the bottle caps. That was so long ago. Decades of people, experiences and scenarios had come and gone since then. Why remember this insignificant vignette? For a moment, he considered if this was how dementia or Alzheimer's started. He imagined his brain cells pushing and shoving, with those storing older memories rising from the depths and bullying their way to the surface. He smiled. That wouldn't be so bad, he thought. Most days, he preferred the memories.

Frank was still playing with the image of a cerebral scrimmage when he reached the diner. He opened the door, felt the rush of air-conditioning on his face, and looked around to see if the Saturday lunch crowd had arrived yet. Not too crowded, he thought with a twinge of guilt; he wanted business to be good for the couple who owned the restaurant, but he didn't enjoy his lunches nearly as much when they were too busy to talk to him. Lunch had become a ritual for him in the last two years, eating here weekdays, plus Saturdays. People, sports, politics—there wasn't much he and Bill hadn't covered. He headed toward an empty bar stool where he would find a better chance for conversation with his friend behind the counter.

"Hey, Frank." A woman's voice spoke from behind him. "I was hoping you'd come early today. We have all your favorites on the menu and I hoped you'd come in before we ran out." Short and in her late 40s, Mary Simmons was a no-nonsense sort who knew her customers and more often than not told them what to order and when to leave. But no one minded. Other than the occasional newcomer or Vols fan in for the UT football game, her customers came here as much for the amiable owners as they did for the food.

Frank took off his hat and Mary gave him a half-hug, putting her arm around the older man in a way that suggested a long-standing friendship. "How's your knee today? Better? Good. Go see Bill. I'll pop over in a minute as soon as I get these folks settled." She hustled away, giving her attention to a booth of two animated couples.

Diners looked up as the white-haired man made his way to the left end of the L-shaped counter. Some smiled, waved, or said hello. A few stared curiously, noticing his hat hung by the door and his dated seersucker suit. Frank nodded at his acquaintances and ignored the strangers. He had long ago stopped caring what others thought of him. Life—his anyway—was too short to fret over the trivial stuff. Truth be told, the only thing that bothered him today was his aching knee.

At the far-right end of the counter, a young woman watched as he came in, greeted other diners, and then gingerly settled his body on a red vinyl bar stool, balancing an old-fashioned wooden cane against the counter. Weird clothes, she thought, from his hat down to the brown socks and sandals. She had only seen straw hats and suits like that in old movies. The pockets on his jacket sagged, the fabric stretched from years of hands shoved into them. As she watched him, Sara Wright smiled to herself, thinking she was the one usually being stared at. Not so much for her looks, but rather for the style of clothes she chose to wear—a mixture of hippie, grunge, and Goth.

She turned her attention to the grilled cheese sandwich and glass of water in front of her. What was she doing here, anyway? Frowning, she picked the dill pickles from her sandwich and chewed them slowly, absent-mindedly studying the strange man. As she watched, a nervous, plainly dressed middle-aged woman slipped out of the booth where she was eating alone and walked over to him. They spoke in whispers and he appeared to be assuring her of something. She nodded, hesitated, then impulsively kissed his cheek and quickly went back to her booth. The cook behind the counter looked away, pretending not to have witnessed the scene while making a mental note to tell Mary later that Frank had a new admirer. The older man cleared his throat, his cheeks flushing, and idly straightened the silverware on the counter.

Sara cut her sandwich into quarters, letting the melted cheese ooze out while she dreamily created stories about the man. He was probably the owner of the café, or the town's mayor, or maybe some rich, eccentric local character who dressed in worn-out old clothes while stuffing fortunes under his mattress. She was glad to think of something other than her own misery.

Bill, both cook and owner, piled Frank's plate with a double helping of fried okra, meatloaf, mashed potatoes, and a cornbread muffin. "Oh, by the way," he said, "I finished three boxes. Do you really think you can find a buyer for them?" He glanced across the room to be certain his wife was out of earshot. "Mary still doesn't know a thing about this. It's been tricky keeping her out of the basement, but I want to surprise her."

"Absolutely. I have a good feeling about it. Your work is excellent, and I'm sure they're going to love the boxes."

The diner did fairly well, but like so many mom-and-pop businesses, it struggled to compete with the franchise establishments. For months, Frank had encouraged Bill to market his woodworking projects, for recognition as well as for extra income. His latest project was a series of band saw boxes. Each was a work of art, with intricate wood grain designs and curious carved embellishments. Making them even more unusual was that they were made from persimmon wood, the dense hardwood found in the Southeast. Frank knew if he could just get Bill's work in the right venue, it would sell at a high price.

For the next twenty minutes, Frank ate and the two talked on, the stream of their conversation unaffected by frequent interruptions as Bill took and prepared orders and as Frank spoke to diners who stopped to see him on their way in or out of the café.

Sara watched for a little while longer, then looked at her check, fished a few dollars from her jeans pocket and put them on the counter. Bill walked over and took her money. He politely nodded to the girl and watched as she pulled a heavy backpack on her shoulders, picked up a duffle bag from the floor, and walked out of the restaurant. He frowned, wondering what gave such a pretty young girl such a grim look.

***

Burton set the last cardboard box on the floor and looked around at the shop, cluttered now with open boxes and dozens of odd shaped packages wrapped in brown paper. He heard sounds of boxes falling in the sparsely furnished apartment above, followed by a stream of profanity. He would talk to his partner later about the cussing—and lay down some rules while they were in this hick town. All it would take would be one or two deals here, and then they could set up somewhere decent. Or part company, which would be all right with him. Meanwhile, this would have to do. He looked around. The leasing company had arranged to have the metal clothing racks removed, the walls painted, and a couple of partitions brought in. All they had to do was hang up a few canvases in fancy frames and be patient. Yes, this would do just fine.

***

Deer Creek was all abuzz. Getting any new business in a small town these days was huge, but this one was especially interesting to Jessie because it was an art gallery. Marilyn Foster met the owner when he signed the lease at Foster Realty, and she quickly spread the word about the lease and the leasee—three months' cash in advance from a man and his partner. Marilyn had emphasized the word "partner" and thrown out her hand in an affected manner so no one would miss her meaning. The good ol' boys who gathered in the hardware store each week must be scratching their heads, thought Jessie, gazing into the storefront window with the "Coming Soon – Gallery" sign.

Jessie wasn't naïve. It was hard enough for businesses selling daily necessities to make a profit in a small town. There was too much competition from the larger towns nearby, not to mention the big-box stores that were now an eyesore by the interstate exit. She didn't see how a small community like hers could possibly support an art gallery. Still, she hoped it would last. The actual Deer Creek might be running strong, but the town was drying up.

She had taken the long way home so she could see how close the gallery was to opening. Now, breathing hard, she wished she'd waited until another day. The canvas bag of books Karen gave her this morning was growing heavier by the minute. As she looked in the window, she thought she saw movement inside. She opened the door, anxious to welcome the owners to Deer Creek.

"Hello?" Jessie announced herself to an empty room. The place was hardly a gallery yet—more like a storeroom with boxes stacked against the walls. Smaller boxes were piled on top of the old sales counter left from the dress shop that had closed last year. There was a faint odor of fresh paint. She sighed, remembering how it used to be. In her mind, she could still see women flipping through racks of dresses and chatting about their husbands and children, as though all their lives would go on endlessly and unchanging. The clothes were gone now, and so were many of the people, too.

No one answered, but Jessie was sure she had seen someone. Maybe he'd gone to the rear to get another box. She put her tote bag on the floor against the counter and headed toward the back, where the dressing room was. She'd been friends with the dress shop owner for years and knew every square foot of the building.

"Good afternoon." A well-dressed man in his late 30s suddenly came through the curtained doorway behind the counter. "As you can see, we're not quite open for business." The man spoke courteously, working to hide his annoyance. He wasn't ready to start dealing with the locals. He glanced at her faded cotton blouse and baggy knit pants and doubted she could afford anything he had to sell.

"Oh, hello," she said, taking a step back. "Yes, I can see you're not open yet. I just wanted to welcome you to our town and wish you success with your gallery."

"Thank you, ma'am," he said. "I'm Burton Roberts. I'm the owner. I do hope you'll come back when we open, hopefully this coming Friday."

"Burton, where the hell is…?" A shorter, thinner man pushed back the curtains but stopped in mid-sentence when he saw the elderly woman. The gallery owner frowned, but looked at the woman with a forced smile. "And here's my partner, Harris Matthews." The other man grimaced.

"It's nice to meet you both. I'm Jessie Cunningham, and I live on the next block over," she said, gesturing to the back of the building, "actually, just behind your shop." The men said nothing and Jessie felt a little awkward. They might know art, but they didn't know the art of conversation, she thought, and they were definitely going to need that if they planned on making any money here. She waited a few seconds. The owner's associate turned and wordlessly disappeared into the back. The taller man scowled and again forced a smile. "I'm sorry, we've been moving things in for two days, and I guess we're more tired than I realized. But please come back next week. We'll post a sign outside when we're open."

"Of course," said Jessie. "Well then, I'll be running along and let you get back to your work. Good luck." *You're going to need it*, she added silently as she hurried out, disappointed and flustered.

A peculiar anxiety overtook her, and with it an energy that carried her briskly the short distance around the block and to her house. In the old days, she would have just left through the back door of the dress shop, crossed the alley, and gone through the back gate into her own yard. Those days were definitely gone.

She was hot and winded by the time she reached her front door. When she got inside, she put down her purse and keys and walked over to the couch. "Gracie, how's my favorite kitty?" Jessie affectionately petted the mass of gray fur curled up against a pillow. The cat purred in reply, but put a paw over her closed eyes, signaling a preference for sleep. "So, no conversation here either," Jessie said, then walked into the dining room.

It actually hadn't been a dining room for a couple of years, but she still thought of it that way. It was her favorite room in the house. She switched on the light and sat down, eager for the comfort she found within these walls. After Anthony died, Jessie gave their daughter the dining room furniture, moved her large round coffee table into the room, and bought three comfortable brown suede chairs to sit around it. Then she hung paintings all over the walls, paintings done over the years by her husband. Her friends told her she was being overly sentimental, that she was making a shrine to her husband, and tried to dissuade her. But she'd persisted, rearranging the artwork until she had the pieces just the way she wanted them. Francis (she had never called him Frank) was the only one who had encouraged her. In fact, he had insisted on bringing over some men to install special lighting—"museum quality," he had said. And what a difference it had made. He also had several of the paintings reframed. She didn't feel it was necessary. They were all beautiful to her; but, as usual, Francis was right. The new frames enhanced the artwork just as the lighting added drama. Little spotlights hung inches from the ceiling, each directing a soft glow on select places within each painting. Now it was a perfect place to sit and enjoy company—even if the only company was a memory. Looking around the room, surrounded by brilliant colors and designs from more than three dozen paintings, she could feel her mood lighten.

A knock on the door startled her from her thoughts. Reluctantly she went to the front door and opened it, surprised to see the man from the art gallery standing behind her screen door.

"Hello again. I remembered you said you lived just behind the gallery."

"Yes?" said Jessie, puzzled at his presence.

"I believe this belongs to you. You left it by the counter." He held out her canvas bag.

"Oh. I hadn't even missed it. Thank you for bringing it over," she said politely, pushing open the screen door to take her bag. As he moved to hand it to her, he looked past her, his eyes scanning the room in an unconscious habit. It was the surprisingly contemporary and colorless living room that first caught his attention; just as quickly, his gaze was drawn to the vivid reds and blues in the next room.

Without realizing it, Burton came through the doorway, bag still in hand, oblivious to Jessie as she awkwardly stepped aside. Staring, he walked through the small living room into the adjoining room. "Amazing," he said quietly, turning from one wall to the next, trying to absorb it all at once. The styles and sizes of the paintings—obviously not prints—varied widely. A few looked like excellent copies of Monet, but there were other styles in addition to the Impressionism. Two reminded him of Picasso's Blue Period, and one looked like an Andrew Wyeth. But the canvas that caught his breath was centered on the only wall not broken by a doorway or window. Softly but prominently lit and richly framed was a painting that looked very familiar. If he had seen it in a museum he would have said it was a Chagall. *A Chagall.* But surely not here, in this house, in this town. It was impossible.

"Where did you… how did you get… what…?" He turned and looked at Jessie in wonder. He hadn't meant to come inside. He only wanted to bring her books over so she wouldn't return for them. Once at her doorway, he expected to see stuffy old furniture dotted with doilies. But this? This was magnificent.

"My husband loved art," Jessie said simply, a frown forming as she realized that she didn't like this stranger, and she didn't want him looking at Anthony's art. Usually she loved talking about the paintings and invited admirers to sit and enjoy them. But this man had made a bad first impression on her, and she didn't want to share her treasures with him. Burton's gaze went back to the Chagall-like painting. He couldn't see a signature. He quickly glanced at two others, also remarkably like Chagall's work. None appeared to be signed.

"Your husband was an artist—or a collector?" He used the past tense because she had.

"He painted some, he collected some." Jessie took her bag from his hand and walked out of the room, talking as she headed to the front door. "I appreciate your bringing me the books. I know you're terribly busy trying to get your shop ready to open, and it was nice of you to come by." She put her hand on the screen door handle, waiting for him to leave.

Burton pulled himself away and went to the door, looking back once. He said goodbye and left, knowing he would be back. Of course, none could be authentic, but the paintings were good.

As good as some forgeries he'd seen. And the one that looked like a Chagall? "*He collected some,*" she had said. He'd have to find out more about this woman and her apparently dead husband. Perhaps she wasn't what she seemed.

***

Sara had been walking down the sidewalk and back for about twenty minutes and now was back in front of the café where she'd eaten. She looked around, as if the buildings themselves could tell her which way to go. Maybe back down the street to the gas station. Maybe Alex had come back and was waiting there for her now, or asking the attendant if she had left a message for him saying where he could find her. *Yeah, right,* she thought. *Like that's going to happen. I waited four and a half hours last night sitting in front of that station, then spent most of my cash on a motel room. And now what? No car, I'm running out of money, and I don't know anyone in this entire state.* For the millionth time, she mentally kicked herself for leaving her credit cards behind. She rarely changed purses, but when she and Alex had gone out three nights ago, she switched a few things from her shoulder-bag to a small clutch. That night was when things started spiraling out of control. It was just luck that she had her birthday money stashed in her backpack when she left with Alex.

Just then, the door swung open and the funny man with the straw hat and cane walked out, bumping into her and almost losing his balance. "Oh, I'm terribly sorry," he said, trying not to stare at the girl's hair. He'd never seen anyone with hair like that. Coal black, shoulder-length, with bangs. Blue bangs. The girl mumbled that it was okay, and started walking away.

He was going to say more, but was interrupted from behind by a booming voice. "Frank Cunningham." The voice belonged to a muscular man in khaki work clothes. "I need to talk to you." Then he lowered his voice and the two moved out of the doorway and talked earnestly for several minutes. Sara had stopped at the shop next to the café, pretending to look interested in the window display but trying to hear what they were saying. She couldn't explain to herself why she was doing it. These people—strangers—were of no concern to her. Yet she was curious about the older man. He seemed to know everyone, and they all wanted to talk to him. She found that intriguing, as though she were watching a movie or TV show. Or maybe, she told herself, she wanted to escape her own life for the moment, so anyone else's life was more interesting. For whatever reason, she hung around pretending to window-shop until the men finished talking and the man called Frank Cunningham ambled away. She stood silent on the sidewalk perhaps a minute, then she followed him.

***

Frank leisurely walked the four blocks back to his house, his cane tapping the sidewalk. He felt lucky to live within walking distance of the café, the old hardware store, and the barber shop. When he was younger, it was normal for city folks to live that way.

Then there was the mass rush to the suburbs, and the inner-city neighborhoods suffered for many years. He and his wife held on through the ups and downs of urban development and now their little neighborhood was trendy, just steps from what had become known as the historical district. "I'm somewhat historical myself," he said, then sheepishly looked around to see if anyone had heard him talking to himself.

He saw the girl he'd bumped into in front of the café, the girl with the blue hair, about a block behind him. He wondered where she was going and tried to recall if he'd seen her here in his neighborhood before. Surely he would have remembered her, with that hair and makeup, and he wasn't positive, but he thought he'd glimpsed some piercing on her face. He shook his head, puzzled as to why anyone would want to poke holes in their face. Finally, he was at his front porch. And not a moment too soon, he thought. He was hot and out of breath and his knee was throbbing. *I'm getting old,* he told himself as he went inside.

***

Sara was careful not to follow too closely. She stopped occasionally to set down the duffel bag and look at the flyer she'd picked up outside one of the shops, hoping that if anyone was watching her from behind the curtained and shuttered windows, they would think she was following directions. She saw the man go into a brown brick house with a covered porch. She walked past the house, trying not to be obvious as she stole a few glances.

She kept going toward the corner, counting how many houses there were between his and the bus stop at the intersecting street. Rounding the corner, she saw that the houses she'd passed were backed by an old gravel service road. She looked up the alley, counted four houses from the corner and there it was, the brown brick house. She turned back to the bus stop, dumped her bags on the bench, and sat down. *If I blow the rest of my cash on another motel room, I won't have any money left. There's no one I can call to come get me—or no one who would come after the way I treated them—and no one knows where I am. Well, no one but Alex. Think. You've just aced three years of college, you're not stupid. You can get out of this mess and get back home. You just need a little time, a plan, and maybe some help.* She sat for almost an hour, loaded up again, got her bearings, and began walking. *One block up, make a left, walk another block, go left, walk half a block.* When she came to the service road, she stopped and cautiously looked around her. No one was out. She took a deep breath and started walking down the alley.

2. SUNDAY

Click. Click. Frank sighed. He turned the key again, muttering words of encouragement, but the engine gave him nothing in return. Cars filed past him, jockeying to beat one another out of the church parking lot, brotherly love seemingly left behind with the bulletins that sprinkled the church pews.

He waited a few minutes and tried again, berating himself for not knowing more—okay, anything—about the machinery under the hood. He was debating the cost of a tow truck when someone opened the passenger side door. He was rescued.

"You look like you could use a hand."

"Sam, am I glad to see you. I guess it's the battery."

"I'll bring my truck around and give you a jump."

In no time, the engine was humming. "I really appreciate this, Sam. Can I buy you a cup of coffee?"

"Thanks, but no," the man replied, nodding to the woman sitting inside his truck and tapping her watch. "We're headed out to see the grandkids, and you know how that daughter-in-law of ours is. Sunday dinner is on the table at 12:30 sharp. Actually, we were looking for you after church. We stopped by your place this morning but didn't have time to ring the bell, because as usual, the missus was running late. I put some tomatoes from my garden on your porch. And some apples from the farmer's market. Martha bought too many, and we thought you might enjoy them."

"A couple of brownies, too," his wife added, leaning out the truck window. The men shook hands and Frank headed home, his mouth watering at the thought of home-grown tomatoes. The kind in the grocery store never tasted as good as home-grown. He'd read somewhere that store tomatoes were picked green and then gassed with ethylene to make them turn red. Or was it to keep them from ripening too fast? Or was ethylene a naturally occurring process? He'd have to look it up sometime. He kept an ongoing list in his head of things to look up. But when he sat down at his computer and logged on to the Internet, he usually forgot what was on his list. No matter. Most weren't important enough to remember anyway.

Frank backed into his driveway so his car would be facing forward, just in case he needed another battery jump. He added to his mental list to look up the price of a new battery.

On the porch, he looked around for the sack. He saw his newspaper but no sack. He unlocked the door and walked through the house to the back porch. Nothing there either. Odd, he thought, shaking his head. Maybe Sam left them at the wrong house.

He grinned as he recalled an incident last December when Sam actually went to the wrong house. Martha had called and asked if they could cut some magnolia branches from his tree for holiday decorations. He said sure, but Sam never came. He found out later that Sam stopped at a house a block over and cut an armful of branches before the owner stormed out and demanded to know what he was doing. Eventually the man laughed about it and wished him a Merry Christmas, but Sam was so embarrassed he went straight home and refused to help Martha with any of the decorations.

Maybe Sam went to the other house again? No, Martha was with him today. Or maybe the couple was confused—they were getting on in years, after all. He dismissed it and went back to the front porch to get his Sunday *New York Times*. Normally he didn't indulge himself with extravagances, but the newspaper was an exception he looked forward to every weekend.

Frank opened the front door and stopped in his tracks. The girl with the blue hair was on his porch with a sack in her arms. She looked as surprised as he was.

"I…I…I'm sorry, I'm so sorry," she said, clutching the bag tightly. Her chin quivered and her voice was shaky. "I'll pay you for what I ate, some apples and brownies…I really am sorry. I came to your door this morning and you weren't home and I saw this, and I don't know why I took it—I've never stolen anything before in my whole life. Please don't call the police."

Frank wasn't quite sure what to make of her. She looked genuinely scared, but she also looked a little scary, and somewhat like a character on a cop show he'd seen on TV last night. But there was something honest about the way she looked him straight in the eye. So she took the tomatoes; it wasn't as though he'd caught her stealing his wallet.

"Young lady," he started sternly, then abruptly stopped and looked longingly at the sack she was gripping. "Are there tomatoes left?" She quickly handed over the sack; he looked inside, where five huge tomatoes gleamed a ripe red. "I have no intention of calling the police," he finally said. "One, they've got better things to do, and two, my mouth has been watering for a tomato sandwich and I don't want to waste any more time talking about it." He saw the confusion and uncertainty in her face. She looked lost. Impulsively, he added, "Come inside and we'll settle this while I fix us some lunch." With that, he stepped back and held the door open, motioning for her to go inside.

Stunned, Sara obediently went into the house, stepping into a cluttered living room and the noisy hum of a window unit air-conditioner. She watched him close the storm door, hesitate, and pull the heavy wooden door all the way open. The layout of the house offered a clear view from the street straight through to the back of the house. She wondered if the open door was to make her feel safer, or him.

Minutes later, they sat facing one another across an old yellow Formica table, each silently and hungrily eating a tomato sandwich. He partnered his tomatoes with onion slices on white bread slathered with peanut butter—a combination Sara politely declined. Hers was simply sliced tomatoes with mayonnaise on both bread slices. It was a summer treat she and her dad ate when she was growing up. The memory made her homesick, but it didn't quell her appetite. She nearly inhaled the sandwich. Yesterday, she'd eaten only the grilled cheese at the café, and this morning she'd scarfed down two apples and four brownies. Energized by the food, she gave the man a grateful smile. She needed someone she could turn to. Maybe this strange old guy would help her.

Frank finished his sandwich and wiped his hands and mouth

with a torn paper towel. When Emmie was alive, they used cloth napkins. Afterwards, he bought paper napkins, folding one each night and putting it under his fork when he prepared his dinner. That seemed senseless after a while. Now he just used paper towels, and lately he tore each one in half, saving part for the next meal.

As he watched the girl eat, he wondered what her story was. It was obvious that she was hungry, yet she didn't look poor. Her hair—strange as it was—was stylishly cut, and her clothes were clean and reminded him of what some of the local kids wore. Those things alone didn't mean much, but the girl had the healthy look of a person who had eaten nutritiously for a lifetime, and her teeth were nearly perfect, probably the product of a few years of braces. Frank knew people from all walks of life, many down on their luck. People who regularly skipped meals so their children could eat, who didn't go to salons to have their hair trimmed, who couldn't afford designer jeans, who never saw a dentist. Whoever this girl was, she had not been living on the streets.

"Now," said Frank, "let's talk. My name is Frank Cunningham. What's your name?"

"Sara."

"Sara…?

"Sara Wright."

"Okay, Sara Wright, after we bumped into one another yesterday at the café, I saw you on the sidewalk when I was walking home." He saw a flicker of surprise in her eyes and continued. "Do you live around here? Or were you following me?"

"No…I mean yes…I mean, I wasn't really following you. And I don't live here, I was supposed to be going to Chicago with a friend, but he..." She looked down, partly angry and partly humiliated. "We split up down at the BP station a few blocks from here. My cell phone, uh, fell out of my bag and was run over by a truck at the gas station and I couldn't call anyone to come get me. I saw how people acted toward you yesterday at the diner and then on the street, and I thought this morning that I could talk to you and that maybe, well, you know, maybe you could help me." There, she'd said it, and he wasn't laughing at her or yelling at her. She was mad at herself—and a little mad at him—because he so easily had gotten that much out of her. She waited for his reaction.

"I see," he lied. He didn't know quite what to make of her. She certainly wasn't timid. And she had definitely gotten past her fear and embarrassment at being caught red-handed on his porch. Also she sounded truthful—not totally truthful, he could see that much. There was a bigger story there.

He spoke with caution, taken aback by the impression she had of his encounters yesterday. "I don't know what I can do to help you, but I'll try. I need to know something first. Are you in trouble with the police?" He couldn't afford to get involved in that kind of situation.

"Of course not!" she said indignantly. "I told you I'd never taken anything before. And it was just two apples."

Frank held up his hands. "All right, all right. I believe you. And I'll try to help. You can use my phone to call your parents. Where do they live?"

"It's just my dad, and he's out of the country for a while," she said, evading his question. "There's no point in calling him."

"I see," he lied again. "Then how about calling a friend? There must be someone you can call."

Sara felt her cheeks burn, recalling the bitter arguments she'd had with her friends who had only tried to warn her about Alex. She was too ashamed and embarrassed to call them now. She inhaled and looked squarely at Frank. "No, there's not. I thought maybe you could help me find a job or something, so I could earn enough money to fly home."

He returned her gaze. The girl did have spunk. He'd give her that. Still, she was delusional to think that she—or he—could immediately secure a temporary job that would pay enough money for an airline ticket. His instincts were right. She must be from a well-to-do family. No one on the streets would dare to think it was that easy to find quick work that paid well, not anything legitimate, anyway.

"Jobs aren't too plentiful around here—or anywhere for that matter. What about a credit card? You could just charge a plane ticket. I'll drive you to the airport."

Sara shook her head. "I have credit cards, but not with me. When I packed, I put my keys and my purse in my backpack, but Alex was in a hurry to leave, and… I forgot that I had changed purses and didn't have everything."

Changed purses? Frank found that puzzling. Why would a woman change purses? He didn't remember Emmie ever doing that, except when her old one wore out. That must be something young women did. Whatever the reason, it certainly hadn't worked out for this one. Despite her sassy attitude, she looked miserable. Frank thought it was more than forgetting her credit card, though. Probably that Alex person.

"Tell you what," he said. "There's a little room in the garage that my son used to stay in when he thought he was too grown-up to live here anymore. You can stay there for a couple of days, maybe do some odd jobs around here for me while we figure out what to do, or at least until you can reach your father. Help me clean up this, and I'll show you where you can stay."

Sara couldn't believe it. She was so relieved. She could feel her eyes getting teary and she blinked quickly so he wouldn't see. "Thank you, Mr. Cunningham. I don't know what to say."

"Call me Frank."

They worked quickly and quietly, washing their plates and knives and wiping off the table, each keeping an arm's length from the other in an odd dance of cooperation and wariness. He was sincere when he said he would try to help her but he also was leery. He didn't want this to turn into a spot on the evening news: foolish man living alone takes in runaway, is robbed and murdered in his kitchen, leaving a plate of ripe tomatoes uneaten.

Meanwhile, Sara was lost in her own thoughts, thinking about the mess she'd apparently made of her life as well as her current situation. Until a few months ago, she'd done and said all the things she was supposed to do and say—not because she had to but because she wanted to. She never felt the need to rebel against her father or the lives they led. Then she met Alex, alienated her friends, and had argued non-stop with her dad. Now she was in a stranger's house, and every warning she ever heard told her she should get away as fast as she could. But at the moment, she had nowhere to go. And those people in the diner seemed so, well, *adoring*. He must be okay.

"Uh, Sara," he said from behind her. "There is one thing you could do for me to earn some money while you're here." Sara froze. Fear gripped her and she suddenly had a sick feeling in her stomach. *Dear God,* she thought, *please don't let him be a pervert.*

"I was just wondering... do you cook?"

Sara let out a deep breath. *Thank you, God!* She turned and faced the man. "I can cook some."

"Fried chicken? Meatloaf?" he asked hopefully.

"I'm a vegetarian. I don't eat meat—or cook it."

Frank's face fell. "Oh. Well, at least I have the tomatoes."

***

Frank opened the side door to the garage and found the light switch. He surveyed the small room that had been his son's refuge. It wasn't really an apartment, more a little boy's clubhouse that had morphed into livable quarters, complete with a ratty futon and a coffee table from Goodwill, a chest of drawers from a neighbor that his son had painted purple, and a tiny but mostly functional bathroom that Frank and his son had installed themselves. The window air-conditioner hadn't been turned on since last summer when his son's own son played there, and the room could use a good cleaning. He was about to explain this to Sara when he saw a backpack and duffle bag on the futon. Two well chewed apple cores sat on the old coffee table. Sara blushed, then blurted, "It was unlocked. I know I shouldn't have, but I was going to tell you this morning."

Frank sighed. This might be more difficult than he had thought.

***

After the confusion of the morning, Frank looked forward to spending the next hour or so lazily reading his Sunday *Times*. He usually read it in the coolness of the living room, but today he headed to the back porch, the bulky paper in one hand and a glass of tea in the other. From there, he could see when the girl came out of the garage.

He sat down in one of two oversized patio chairs on his screened porch and opened his paper, methodically pulling out the sections he wanted to read and putting the rest on the floor. A wasp hit the screen and Frank looked up. He gazed dreamily, wondering who had invented the wire mesh that kept the bugs out but let the breeze through. His mind wandered to the trip to France that Emmie and he had taken three years ago. Or was it four, even five? He smiled at the remembrance. The wasp hit the screen again and he thought about the place they'd stayed at in France with its unscreened windows and how he'd laughed at her fussing about the bugs. He shook his head, as if to bring himself back to the present, and turned his attention to the newspaper. *Reading the paper has become a lost art,* he thought. *Most people now get the news from TV and the Internet. A hundred years ago, people would stand and listen to orators for hours. Now they have the attention span of a goldfish and communicate in 48 characters or less. We've stopped evolving. Pretty soon, man will go back to just burping and farting.* He flicked the paper with annoyance, thinking, *Emmie would understand.*

Frank stopped. He knew if he let himself, he would start reminiscing, and he made himself concentrate on the paper instead. He would save his thoughts of her for tonight. Sometimes if he thought intently about Emmie before he went to sleep, he would dream of her. Those were the best nights. Once he dreamed she called him on the phone. In his dream, they were thrilled that they had found a way to communicate again, after death. He woke the next morning still hearing her voice, so real, so alive. Now each night he hoped the dream would return. So far, it had not.

Frank spent the next hour reading, occasionally tearing out an article he would save for Bill. The porch was hot, and his reading and the hum of the insects outside made him drowsy. He was about to doze off when he heard Sara come out of the garage. She started up the driveway toward the front door. "I'm back here," he called to her. She turned and walked to the back porch door, tentatively opening the screen door. "Have a seat. I was just reading the paper."

"I thought maybe we could talk about what kind of work I could do to make some money. You know, so I can get out of he… out of your way."

"Of course, of course, I know you want to get home," Frank said. "I'll make some calls for you tomorrow. It being Sunday, I don't think I could reach anyone today. What sort of skills do you have? I mean, what is your training, or your education? What kind of jobs have you had before?"

"I'll be a senior in college this fall, and I'm majoring in psychology."

"Psychology? Really?"

"Well, yes, what's wrong with that?" she asked defensively.

Frank took a deep breath. One minute she seemed frightened and insecure and the next minute she was snapping at him.

"There's nothing *wrong* with it, I just expected something different, maybe art or literature, or..."

"Or what, astrology? Basket-weaving? You think I'm an airhead, don't you?" Sara stood up and backed toward the door. "I'm not stupid. I'm smart. I make A's in school, and just because I don't look like you think I should look doesn't mean I'm not as good as..."

"Whoa! Hold on there, Sara. Please. Sit down. I just thought that based on your, um, alternative style, you probably had chosen a less traditional line of study. That's all. I can see I was wrong. Now, regarding work," he said, eager to change the subject, "what sort of experience have you had?"

Sara relaxed a little and sat down across from him. "I've done some office work, you know, typing, filing, and I was an intern last summer at a social services office." She stopped, then added, "I wasn't going to work this summer. My father was taking me with him on a trip... a trip related to his job. It was going to be my last fun summer before I got out of school and went to work full-time. But that didn't work out." She looked like she wanted to explain more, but didn't.

"Hmmm," Frank murmured, "I haven't seen many job listings lately, either in the newspaper or online."

Sara looked at him strangely, wondering why he would be looking for a job at his age. Instead, she pointed to the newspaper on the table. "Were you looking for jobs in there?"

Frank shook his head, amused. "Oh, no, no, no. There won't be any local jobs in here. This is the *New York Times*. Our local paper didn't come today. They must have another new delivery person on the route. But even if we had it here, it wouldn't have much. Probably like your own city's newspaper, they put most of the listings online. I get the *Times* just on Sunday," he added, "and they hardly ever list jobs in the editions delivered out of state. See," he said, holding up a thin section, "they just list a handful." His eyes scanned the page, trying to imagine what the listings looked like in the editions printed for New York's readers. He was sure they had shrunk like the listings in his own city's paper.

"I've never looked for a job in a newspaper," Sara said, trying to sound as if she'd hunted for and held a number of jobs. He didn't have to know that she'd only had two summer jobs, plus of course the usual baby-sitting jobs through high school that most girls had. "I thought all the good jobs were only listed online." When Frank didn't respond, she looked up, expecting him to make some disparaging comment about computers. He had an odd look on his face and was staring at the newspaper. "What is it? Did you find me a job in New York?" she joked.

"What? Oh, I'm sorry, I just saw the strangest thing." He folded the newspaper page in half, then in half again. "There's an ad in here about a job in Deer Creek." He looked up at Sara. "That's about an hour from here, where my sister-in-law lives. This ad is for a manager of a nature preserve. But I've never heard of this. Deer Creek is a very small town, and there's no nature preserve there."

"Maybe it's new," Sara said. "Or maybe it was there before but now has a new name." He didn't respond. To break the silence, she asked what the ad said.

"Manager. Deer Creek Nature Preserve," he read. *"Immediate*

opening for supervisor of 504-acre sanctuary. Must have degrees in Botany and Wildlife Management. 12 years' experience required. Typical relocation package. P.O. Box 64876, Deer Creek, TN. Attn: Charles Gallager. Very odd. You're probably right, it must be something new. But I think I'll call my sister-in-law, and satisfy my curiosity. I'll be right back."

He went into the house, taking the folded newspaper sheet with him.

After he left, Sara killed a little time looking at the newspaper. Frustrated and bored, she tossed it aside and walked outside. She looked past the yard to the alley she'd crept down less than twenty-four hours ago. Was it really possible that she could get a temp job here, or maybe even work in that café for a little while? Maybe she could make enough to buy a plane ticket home. Or, if she could just make enough to support herself until her dad and his "friend" got back, she could call home and get him to buy her a ticket. As she thought of her dad, she realized she wasn't as angry at him as she had been a few days ago. Things would have been so different if only...

"Sara?" Frank was walking toward her. He looked worried. "Sara, I need to go to Deer Creek. Tomorrow. As soon as I get back, I'll try to help you find some temporary work. I promise. And if I can't," he hesitated, then said, "well, if I can't, I'll drive you home myself. That is, if it's not very far?"

"Savannah."

For a moment, Frank turned from his concern for Jessie and came back to the situation at hand. So, Sara Wright lived in Savannah. He hid his satisfaction. Maybe she would let down her guard and tell him more. If not, at least now he had a name and a city. It wouldn't be hard to find out more. He had to be sure she wasn't a runaway.

They went back inside and into the living room, where Frank picked up a small notebook and quickly wrote inside. At a desk in the corner, he turned on his computer and pulled out the chair for Sara. "Here," he said, "you can check the local help-wanted ads online if you want, but more importantly, you should type up a resume. One page. Unless you have one? No? No problem. It doesn't have to be too detailed. You just need something to give to anyone we can find for you to talk to about working when I get back. You can use my address and phone number. I'll write it down for you." Sara cheerfully went along, thinking that if he was that optimistic, maybe things would work out after all. His computer was sleek, and she saw that his printer and desk phone all looked new. She'd have to remember to ask him what he did, or what he used to do. He must be retired, since he looked fairly old and didn't mention a job. But then, he indicated that he looked for jobs, so maybe he was out of work, or just needed money. The electronics looked new, but both he and his furniture looked a bit shabby to her.

She spent a long time typing, deleting, starting over, and finally was satisfied with her resume. After printing a few copies, she shut down the computer and walked around the living room, looking at photographs and mementos. Somewhat disappointed, she surmised that he was a retired teacher. Not as interesting as she had imagined, but it explained a lot. Probably those people who were fawning over him yesterday were former students. She heard noises from the back of the house and wandered into the kitchen. Frank was looking in the refrigerator. It was only then that she realized she was hungry again, and saw that it was dusk outside.

Frank looked up. "Oh you're finished? Good, good. I thought perhaps I'd fix us some scrambled eggs. Do you eat eggs?"

"Sure. Sounds good. I'll help."

After a few minutes of getting in each other's way, Frank sat down and watched as Sara expertly put together a meal of cheese omelets, sliced tomatoes, and apples baked in the microwave with cinnamon and butter. He didn't keep many groceries on hand, and he was impressed at her resourcefulness.

Once again, they ate in silence, Frank enjoying every bite and Sara thinking about the cabinets full of food she and her dad had back at home. Again, she wondered why this man seemed to live so frugally. Her dad taught at a college, and he made enough money for the two of them to live comfortably. Of course, the computer and printer were expensive-looking, and she'd noticed he had a smart phone. Maybe he just spent his money on electronics.

Sara spoke first. "How long are you going to be gone tomorrow?"

Frank hadn't thought about leaving her here. But he hadn't thought about taking her either. What should he do? Leave her in his house? He felt more comfortable keeping an eye on her.

"Why don't you come with me? If we leave early in the morning, we can be back before dark." When she didn't reply immediately, he spoke again. "The thing is, Sara, my older brother died not too long ago, and before he died, he asked me to look out for his wife. So I call Jessie once a week, and I drive over to see her about every three months or so. When I called her this afternoon, she sounded worried and distracted, very unlike her usual self, and I just saw her a month ago and she was fine. Oh, and I asked about the nature preserve. She had no idea what I was talking about. So I can use that as an excuse for going to see her, so she won't think I'm a busybody."

"Well, I guess I may as well go with you," Sara said tentatively. "I can help with the driving if you want me to. As a way to pay you back for letting me stay here, and for the food."

He smiled. "Great. We'll leave right after breakfast. I'll get you some clean sheets and towels and get you settled out back."

It seemed awfully early to Sara for calling it a day, but she didn't mind being alone. Frank was nice enough—actually, he was extremely nice to let her stay there and to help her—but she looked forward to some alone time. She needed to think, about Alex, about her father, about herself.

When she was sure he was gone, she dug through her backpack, pulled out her cell phone, and turned it on. There were no messages and no missed calls. Not that she had really expected any, but there was always a chance. She told herself again that she was okay with being alone. It was the rejection that tore at her heart. Digging around again, she pulled out her charger, found an outlet for it, and plugged in her phone. She felt a little guilty about lying to Frank. But how could she explain that she had a phone and not one person to call?

***

Frank waited until he heard the girl deadbolt the garage door, then he went back inside, turned off the lights, and went to his bedroom. This time of night was usually the low point in his day, a recurring reminder that his wife was gone, and that despite his family, friends, and activities, he was in the evening side of life.

He wasn't old, he told himself. 90 was old. Even 80. In his 70's, he could easily have another twenty years or more left in him. Maybe more. Lots of people lived to be 100. Every now and then, he would read about someone living to be 110 or older. *Imagine that. If I'm going to live another twenty or thirty years, I'd better make some changes. Better start taking better care of myself.* His knee ached. Walking was supposed to help, but he hadn't felt that he'd made much progress in recent days.

He looked longingly at the photograph of the smiling woman on the dresser. "Emmie," he said out loud, "we may have a new project. You'd like this one. She's different. I think she has potential." He glanced at the torn piece of paper stuck in the corner of the mirror. He thought about opening the frame and putting the slip of paper in with Emmie's photo. But he liked to hold it in his hands. Touch it. Because it was her writing and doodling. On the paper were calligraphy letters decorated with tiny flower designs. Emmie said once she was going to cross-stitch it as a reminder of their little project. There were so many things she was going to do. For the millionth time, he thought of how quickly life can change, or end.

And now there was another person with a problem to contend with: the girl in his garage. He couldn't quite pinpoint his concern. Maybe he was leery of what he didn't know about her.

She was an unknown quantity. He couldn't afford to deal with people who held secrets from him.

In the garage, Sara made up the futon, looked around for spiders, and found some paper towels and cleaner in the bathroom. She wiped off a few surfaces and found that it wasn't terribly dirty, just old and dusty. She saw a basket of toys in the corner that she hadn't noticed the night before, with a coloring book tossed on top. Flipping through it she saw a page with the words "for Grandpa" clumsily written in crayon. Last night, the room felt spooky. Tonight, it seemed homey. It was small, clean enough, and best of all, she could go to sleep without feeling like a criminal for being there. She double-checked the deadbolt, took a quick shower in the tiny bathroom, put on a tee-shirt, checked the deadbolt again, turned off the light and slipped between the cool sheets. It had been a long day, but she had survived. This wasn't the adventure she had planned, but she wasn't sorry. For the moment, she was satisfied—not happy, but not unhappy either. She didn't know what she felt. Sara lay awake for hours, thinking.

3. MONDAY

*Frank looked closely at the young woman dozing in the passen-*ger seat. This was the first opportunity he'd had to really study her without appearing to be rude. Tight jeans, tie-dyed shirt, that garish blue dye in her hair. Too many earrings—were there five in each ear?—a small diamond glittering from the side of her nose. Black eyeliner. Bright metallic blue fingernails on just one hand. A tattoo on the inside of her wrist. He understood that each generation had their own philosophies and fashions, but he didn't understand this look.

She perplexed him. In the less than 24 hours since she'd inserted herself into his life, she had appeared scared, embarrassed, defiant, secretive, helpful, and eager. This morning, she'd been grumpy and sullen. When he reached to put her backpack in the back seat, she refused and held it on her lap in the car. Was he taking a foolish chance? She might be hiding drugs—or a gun—in there. Suppose yesterday was just an act and she wasn't the harmless person she appeared to be?

He'd always thought he could read people, could size up a

person better than most. With some vanity, he thought of it as a gift that carried him through an accomplished university career and some dubious business transactions. Now he depended on it to ensure the success of his current deals. But this girl, well, maybe the age difference was too great for him to read her. It puzzled him.

Sara was waking up. Good. He was nearing the exit he needed to take to stop for gas. A few minutes out of the car would feel good. Arthritis was such a pain. And his knee was swelling again. Dr. Renthrop said the arthroscopic surgery was successful, but how would he know? He wasn't the one limping around. It had been two months and his knee still hurt. Frank started using the cane when they took the crutch away, and now the doctor wanted him to stop using the cane, too. Well, good luck on that one, doc. He'd done those ridiculous exercises, he'd walked every day like was supposed to, and he wasn't giving up his cane until he was good and ready.

Frank took the interstate exit ramp and turned into the gas station, relieved to see a battered red pickup parked over to the side of the station. That meant Jose was working the day shift now. Not only could he check on the young assistant manager, but he could also enlist his help if he needed another jump-start—or any other kind of help. Even as he thought it, he chastised himself for his negative imagination. Sara was just a young woman down on her luck—hardly more than a girl.

Sara jerked awake and looked out the window. "Are we there yet?" Frank found himself relaxing again. Now she seemed more child than woman.

"Almost," said Frank. "It's just a few exits up the road, but we need gas, and I thought you might like a bite to eat. Jessie won't be home for another hour. We're early." *And*, he thought to himself, *maybe you'll look in the restroom mirror and take some of that metal off your face. Poor Jessie isn't always the most tactful person—heart of gold, but tactful? No. Lord knows what she'll blurt out when she sees you.* He parked the car next to one of the many gasoline pumps and popped open the gas tank lid. *Why does everything have to change so?* he wondered. *Rows of gas pumps, all self-service, pushing buttons and paying with a plastic card. I miss the old days when someone pumped your gas, washed your windshield...even checked your oil and tires. Guess that's why they stopping calling them service stations.*

Frank noticed that Sara was looking at him oddly; he hoped he hadn't been talking out loud again.

Sara sat nervously while the older man shuffled around the car. Her head was spinning with the memory of her last gas station stop. After several hours of arguing, she and Alex had stopped for gas. While she was in the station's restroom, he put her bags by the gas pump and drove away. No arrangements to get her back home, no I'm sorry, no goodbye. She could still see the pitying look on the clerk's face. After hanging around for four miserable hours, Sara left a message for Alex with the clerk, and even went back the next morning. But Alex never came back for her. She wondered if he had gone on to Chicago to meet his friends, or without her to help him pay the way, did he go back home himself?

Home. Back at her house there was a note on the kitchen table waiting for her dad to find when he got back. She should have gone with him. It could have been an amazing experience: a month hiking through the mountains and staying in a remote village in Bulgaria of all places. For months, they had planned it as an early college graduation gift. She was going with him on a research trip to the Balkan Mountains. She screwed up that real good. And for what? Alex? They'd started fighting two hours out of Savannah.

She hated him, and she hated herself for being so stupid. She angrily jerked open the car door and got out, taking her backpack with her. "Are you going in?" she asked Frank warily.

"Yes, I'll come in as soon as I finish here, and we'll get a sandwich. We'll be back on the road in no time." He looked at her backpack. "You don't need to carry that in, you know. I'll lock the car."

"I'll take it with me."

Frank wasn't surprised but didn't say anything. He finished pumping the gas and went inside to talk to Jose.

Jose reminded him of his youngest son: independent, fun-loving. The differences ended there, though. Michael had plenty of advantages, had gone to college, got a great job, married a fine girl, and now had his own son. Jose had struggled. His father and brother had gotten caught in the crossfire of a shootout between two gang members. Jose was left to take care of his mother and little sister. He quit high school and bagged groceries to help keep his family afloat. Frank had met him at the grocery store.

One day, Jose told him he'd been approached with an unbelievable offer: six months' rent for free for him and his family if he would study for his GED and enter a community jobs program. It guaranteed a temporary job upon earning his high school equivalency degree, and if he did well for another six months, he would go into a management program. That's where he was now. The teen briefly wondered if Frank were somehow involved, but dismissed the idea in light of the old man's frugal shopping, which always seemed to favor sale items and crumpled coupons.

In the ladies' room, Sara pulled her cell phone out of her backpack and turned it on. The battery was low. She'd have to find a way to discreetly recharge it. If only she hadn't lied about it to start with. And what a ridiculous story, saying a truck ran over her phone. What was the matter with her anyway? She couldn't even lie well. There were no messages, but she wasn't surprised. She turned her cell off and hid it again in her backpack.

When she came out, she saw Frank talking to a young Hispanic man behind the counter. As she watched, she realized they were talking like old friends. It made her think of the people who spoke to him at the café. As they laughed over something one of them said, she wondered if Frank stopped there every time he visited his sister-in-law.

Just then Frank looked up and saw her, all metal still intact. Her hair was combed though and pulled back with something glittery. She looked tense, but when he smiled at her, he thought he caught a trace of a smile in return.

After a snack and a jumpstart from Jose, the two were back on the road. This time Sara was behind the wheel, pleased that he asked her to drive the rest of the way. Maybe she could be his driver for a couple of weeks, she thought. That would be an easy way to make money, and she loved driving, especially away from the traffic of the city. He must not be feeling well, because he had been especially quiet, not speaking much other than to give her directions. Apparently, he had some sort of injury, because the man at the gas station had fixed him an ice bag to hold on his knee. So the cane was temporary. Maybe he wasn't as old as she thought. He also didn't act old. She noticed that he frequently checked his cell phone and texted messages while she drove, probably as much as she used to do.

"Take this exit," he said, pointing to an exit sign ahead. He directed her past more gas stations and fast-food restaurants and into a residential neighborhood. "Pull over here," he said, quickly adding, "but don't turn off the ignition."

Sara parked and began to unbuckle her seat belt. "We're not there yet. I just wanted to say something first," said Frank. "You see, Jessie, my sister-in-law, is a really sweet, kind person. And very trusting." He seemed hesitant. Sara wondered what he was thinking. Since their encounter yesterday, he hadn't mentioned the food she had taken, nor had he reprimanded her for breaking into his garage. Well, it wasn't a real break-in if the door wasn't locked, was it? Maybe just trespassing. What was he getting at now? Did he think she was going to take something from the woman?

"Look, I'm not going to steal anything from her," Sara snapped. "I told you, I've never stolen anything before, not in my whole life. It was just that once."

Perplexed, Frank shook his head. "I wasn't going to say that. I just wanted to tell you that my sister-in-law is a wonderful person but she's a bit quirky sometimes, so if she says anything strange, please just pretend you don't notice, and don't be offended. She has a heart of gold, but can be just a bit, well, like I said, odd."

Sara stared back. Odd? This from a man who wore a straw hat? She shook her head, unable to form a reply. Frank took it for an affirmation and pointed ahead, giving the last directions to Jessie's house.

Minutes later, they parked in front of a modest yellow house with a large front porch and a front yard that needed mowing. Unlike the pristine lawns of his own neighborhood, the grass in Jessie's yard was a kaleidoscope of greens—fescue and clover, Bermuda and dandelions, all dotted with crabgrass. Frank found the unkempt yard comforting. He wondered if children still searched for four-leaf clovers for good luck or tied clover chains to wear around their necks.

He was eager to see Jessie and hoped that whatever was wrong yesterday when he called was over and that she'd be her happy self again. The bond between them was strong, forged though the love and loss of two people. Frank's brother, Tony, had been diagnosed with cancer. Despite chemo and radiation, the doctors said there was nothing more that could be done and had given him only months to live. Frank and Emmie drove over each weekend to visit him. Then, one Friday evening on their way there, their car was hit by a drunk driver. Frank was bruised and cut up a little; Emmie was killed instantly. While he had been consumed with worry over Tony, it was his Emmie that he lost without warning. Tony died three months later. Frank lost his wife and brother. Jessie lost her husband and a dear friend. For two years now, they had grieved both separately and together, unknowingly leaning on one another as they adjusted to the solitary lives neither wanted.

Frank knocked on the door. Sara stood on the bottom porch step, pulling her backpack onto her shoulders.

Jessie opened the door and beamed when she saw Frank. "Francis! Oh, I am so glad to see you!" She hugged him tightly, surprising Frank, and pulled back only when she saw Sara on the steps. She seemed confused. "And who is this?" Jessie looked from Sara to Frank.

Sara glared at Frank. Didn't he tell the woman he was bringing her?

Frank was puzzled, too. "I'm sorry, Jessie, I thought I told you on the phone. This is Sara Wright. Sara is, uh, renting the garage apartment from me for a couple of weeks. And today she's my driver." He rubbed his knee gently, hoping for a little sympathy instead of the looks he was getting from the two women. Jessie again looked from one to the other. Sara had stepped onto the porch and stood, arms folded, facing Frank. It was apparent that something unusual was going on, but Jessie had her own worries. And for the moment at least, she was glad to have company.

"Sara. What a beautiful name for such a beautiful girl," Jessie said, patting the girl's arm and openly gazing at her hair, makeup, earrings, and nose ring. "I love your hair. Francis, you've brought me a rainbow. Have a seat here on the porch and rest from your drive. I'll bring you some iced tea."

They sat down and Jessie went inside for their drinks. Sara wondered at Jessie's rainbow comment. Maybe the woman was a poet, or maybe just a little off. Frank did say she was odd. But she sounded sincere when she commented about her hair, so she didn't think she was making fun of her. Sara stood up impulsively. "I'll go inside to help her."

Frank was bewildered. He was sure he had talked about Sara to Jessie on the phone yesterday. In fact, he was positive. *Maybe that's why Jessie sounded odd. Maybe she's losing her hearing and can't keep up with people's conversations. Yes, that's it. Her hearing is going. Well, that's a relief. She'll get a hearing aid, and then everything will be right again. I do wish she wouldn't call me Francis, though.* He stretched out on the porch glider, putting a worn cushion under his knee. He closed his eyes and let his mind drift. His mother had named both her sons after silent film stars. Tony was named after Antonio Moreno and Frank was named after Francis X. Bushman, both handsome leading men of their time. Bushman's career took a dive when the public found out he was having an affair with one of his co-stars. Moreno had his own sad story: shortly after he and his wife divorced, she died in a car crash. Frank never understood why his otherwise practical-minded mother named her sons after movie stars.

Putting aside his idle daydreaming, he turned his thoughts to Sara and wondered how she and Jessie would get along.

Inside, Sara stood in the dining room, absorbing the contrast between the house's old-fashioned exterior and contemporary interior—and especially the unusual art display. As she slowly moved about the room, she seemed lost in the paintings. Her face softened and her shoulders relaxed. She was entranced. Jessie watched her curiously. "Are you interested in art?" she asked.

"I haven't seen much, except in museums, I mean," Sara replied. "But this is great. They are all so colorful and, umm, kind of exciting, you know? This one is so pretty, and this one is like a fantasy drawing. And there's so much life and movement in this one. Now this one," she said, pointing to a whimsical image of a man and a woman, "is almost erotic, but it's funny, too, and that makes it sweet. Together, they're all so very *interesting*."

Jessie's face lit up. It was just the way she felt about the paintings. She liked this girl.

Sara's gaze lingered on the painting. "There's so much love

here," the girl said, almost to herself, "and laughter." The older woman stood quietly, frozen in memory, and wondered how this young stranger could see so clearly what others missed. She pined for the laughter, and for a moment—like every day for the past two years—she let her heart shatter silently, then stored away her thoughts and poured the tea. With ice softly popping in the glasses, they carried the drinks outside. They sat for a while and the two older people made small talk.

Frank was feeling better. Elevating his knee helped ease the swelling, which helped ease the pain. Jessie and Sara seemed comfortable together, and both looked happy. Well, maybe not happy, but relaxed, and certainly not as edgy as they'd seemed earlier.

"Jessie, remember I asked you if there is a nature preserve around here?" He pulled the torn-out newspaper clipping from his jacket pocket and handed it to her. She read the want-ad and handed it back to him.

"Never heard of it," she said flatly. "But there's a lot of undeveloped land outside of town. It's possible someone sold their land to the state. But 504 acres isn't likely. And what an odd number. Why not just 500?" She frowned, looking past Frank to the street. A silver SUV slowed down in front of her house, then drove on. She was pretty sure it was that Burton Roberts man driving. She stared after the car.

"Someone you know?" asked Frank.

"Someone I wish I didn't know," she answered. Prodded, she told them about her encounters the day before with the town's new shop owners. "Marilyn Foster says they're a gay couple." Frank raised his eyebrows. "Oh, don't look at me that way, Francis. That's not why I don't like them. You know I could care less what color shirt a man wears. It's something else about them that bothers me. I just don't like them."

Sara looked over at the woman, then at Frank, who was looking amused.

"At any rate, why don't you call Gary? He's our newspaper editor now. He would know about that wilderness thing—if you're really interested. I know you, you won't let it go until you've solved your little mystery." Her eyes looked off again, in the direction where the silver car had driven. "How long can you stay?" she suddenly asked.

"A day or two, if it's no bother," he said, glancing at Sara, who was staring at him in disbelief. "Or overnight, at the very least."

"Stay as long as you like. I could use the company."

He was right. Something was definitely wrong. Jessie thrived on her time alone and guarded it jealously, sometimes to the point of annoying him and her own children, who each thought she should pack up and alternate staying with them. But Jessie always said she was fine right where she was, that this was her home, and she had commitments in the community. Her son drove over from Nashville about once a month, and her daughter came less.

Maybe Jessie was ill? Frank didn't think he could bear it if she were sick. The thought surprised him, but he quickly dismissed it. She looked well, just nervous. He would call Gary and satisfy his curiosity about the newspaper ad, make sure Jessie was okay, maybe bring up the possibility of a hearing exam, and then go home in the morning. Then he could find Sara some temp work, and everything would be all right. He was accustomed to getting things done, and none of these tasks seemed too difficult. He just had to set things in motion.

Jessie rose from her chair. "I have some chicken almost thawed. We can have that for supper."

"I'm a vegetarian," Sara said, raising her chin slightly. Jessie looked at the girl's face, defiant again. It was hard not to look at Sara, Jessie realized, wondering if that explained why she wore the piercings, the heavy eye makeup, the blue hair, the blue nail polish. Did people do that because they wanted attention? Jessie couldn't fathom that. Although she loved vivid colors and beautiful fabrics and jewelry, she didn't wear them herself. She preferred to be the observer, not the focus of anyone's attention.

Sara seemed to be waiting for an answer. Was there a question? Oh, yes, dinner. And the girl was a vegetarian. Jessie had raised two children and was a grandmother to three. She could handle Sara. But after all, she thought, it was just chicken, hardly worth an argument. "Okay," she said, "we'll have a vegetarian meal." Frank started to protest, but she stopped him short. "Frances, I'll cook fried chicken for you some other time. Tonight, we'll have vegetables and cornbread sticks. You still eat those, don't you?" She was teasing him.

She'd barely gotten the words out before his senses kicked in. In his mind, he could feel and hear the crunch of the crustiness where the cornbread browned in the iron skillet, and he could see the steam rise from the inside as he broke a corn stick in half. He could make a meal of Jessie's cornbread, and she always cooked it when he visited.

"But I'm out of cornmeal," Jessie said. "Sara, you can drive me up to the Big Star, and Frank, you can go make your phone calls, or just go see Gary." Jessie was now in her element. She loved to cook for her family and friends. The man and girl looked at each other. Apparently they had their assignments, and not sorry to be separated, they agreed.

***

Monday was usually a slow day at Al's Big Star, calm and quiet after the weekend grocery run. Although only a handful of shoppers were there, they all knew Jessie, and they nodded or spoke to her and tried to be discreet when they stared at Sara. Jessie pushed the cart slowly, winding down aisles, telling Sara about the town, the people, and the stores. If she noticed that Sara was silent, it didn't faze her.

"Mommy, look at her! She has BLUE hair!" A child sitting in the grocery cart pointed at Sara and giggled while her mother tried to hush her. "Don't point at people," she said. "Hello, Miss Jessie."

"Hello, Sally. My goodness. It seems like only last week Abby was just a toddler. Now look at her. Oh, don't they grow up fast. Sally, this is my friend Sara. She's visiting me this week."

Friend? Visiting for a week? Sara wanted to object but managed a polite reply, and while the two women talked, she and the child eyed one another. The girl, chocolate fresh on her lips, held out a half-eaten Oreo and offered Sara a bite. Sara grinned and shook her head no. "But thanks anyway."

The girl pointed to Sara's head. "How did you make it blue?"

Before Sara could answer, the girl held up her hand, proudly showing off a stretched out elastic bracelet with dangling beads that would likely never make it out of the store. Sara held up her wrist, and pointed to a design inked on her arm. The girl's eyes grew wide and she glanced at her mother, who was focused on Jessie. She looked back at Sara and with both hands pointed to yellow plastic barrettes in her hair. A piece of Oreo fell to the floor and another piece got caught in her hair. Pulling back her own hair, Sara pointed to her rows of silver earrings. The girl laughed with delight. It was that genuine, innocent laugh that only children can voice, and it made Sara laugh out loud. The sound of her own laughter made her stop—how long had it been since she had laughed? Self-conscious, she looked around her. At the end of the aisle, a policeman was watching her. The women finished their conversation and Jessie directed her cart toward the checkout. As she and the little girl waved goodbye, Sara looked back to where the policeman had been. He hadn't moved. He was young, tan, had a slight frame, and wore his hair in that nearly shaved style that made her think of a soldier. And, he was blatantly watching her.

Jessie paid for her one bag of groceries, chatting nonstop with the clerk. Sara automatically picked up the grocery sack and, matching her pace to Jessie's, walked with her to the car.

"Jessie, wait up." They turned toward the voice and Sara again saw the uniformed man. As he approached, she realized he was wearing a Sheriff's Department uniform, complete with a gun and handcuffs.

"Let me give you a hand with those," he said, taking the groceries from Sara and looking at her with open curiosity.

"Thank you, Mitchell. How have you been keeping? I hardly ever get to see you, but your mom tells me you're doing real well at the Sheriff's office."

Mitch grinned at the older woman. He found her little odd phrases entertaining, maybe because he genuinely liked her and her outspoken manner. Jessie was the only person in town who called him Mitchell. Truthfully, she was the only one he'd let call him Mitchell. "Thanks, Jessie. It's pretty good. For the most part, it's interesting and I like it. I guess I should be glad, but it's been real quiet lately. In fact, the only calls I've had in the last week were complaints from women who say someone's been picking their flowers."

Jessie smiled warmly. "I imagine that will take care of itself before long."

Mitch didn't understand what she meant and instinctively looked at Sara as though she had an explanation. Sara shrugged her shoulders. Lately there were so many things she didn't understand.

"And you are…?" he said.

Sara thought his question borderline rude and decided not to like him. Even if he was cute. Well, not cute like Alex is, or was, or…or what? What did she think of Alex now?

Jessie spoke up. "This is Sara. Sara, this is Mitchell. His mother and I are good friends." She turned back to the young man. "Sara drove Francis over this morning and they're staying for dinner." Her eyes widened, as though she'd just had a revelation. "Why don't you join us? It's just going to be vegetables and cornbread. Just come over at six. There will be plenty, and you can eat and run. I know Francis would love to see you."

Say no, say no, say no, Sara thought, horrified that Jessie might be trying to fix her up with this man.

Mitch looked from one woman to another, then answered. "Thanks, but I can't come for supper... but I will stop by this afternoon if that's all right. It's been a long time since I've seen Frank."

Sara wondered if he had a girlfriend and that was why he refused the dinner invitation. More likely, he was way too conservative to want to join her for dinner. People were so judgmental. Not that she cared, of course. Besides, she would be out of here tomorrow and never be back. Good ol' Frank would help her find some temporary work, even if it was just driving and running errands for him, and she'd be back home before she knew it.

***

Jessie dried her hands on her apron and sighed. She was tired. After living alone, she found that having company was exhausting. "Sara, would you watch the stove while I rest a few minutes?"

"Sure," she replied, eyeing the assortment of pans. "What do you want me to do?"

"Just make sure nothing boils over, but mostly watch the pressure cooker. It'll start to jingle in a few minutes. Let it go for about three minutes and then turn it to low. I'll be back by then. I won't go to sleep. I just need to rest my eyes." Jessie took off her apron and put it across a kitchen chair, thanked Sara, and walked out of the kitchen.

Sara picked up a magazine from the table, flipped through

it, and tossed it aside. She glanced at the pans on the stove and started opening drawers looking for a spoon to stir the vegetables. She stopped in confusion, finding a stack of credit cards and driver's licenses. She picked up the cards and examined them, then shook her head, perplexed. Some were in Jessie's name, or in what must have been her husband's name; but there were other names, too. She shrugged and put them back. She found a wooden spoon, put it on the counter by the stove and looked around the homey kitchen.

She picked up the faded floral-print apron and held it to her waist, wondering what it would be like to have her own house, her own kitchen, her own family to cook for. She'd be successful and wealthy with a great career and a big family. She'd have it all. She tied the apron around her waist behind her back and imagined herself as one of the TV moms she and her best friend used to watch on Nick at Nite. Those families were happy and never had any problems that couldn't be resolved within a half-hour timeslot.

The little round thing on the pressure cooker was beginning to make noises. Sara checked the other two pans and stirred the corn and potatoes. Daydreaming, she imagined herself as Donna Reed, wearing a dress, pearls, and high-heels while cooking a big delicious dinner for her perfect TV family. Those 50s TV shows were unrealistic, she knew, but she loved them. She smiled at the image, holding up the hem of the apron and dancing around the kitchen. Her little dance ended in a twirl, leaving her at the screen door and face-to-face with Jessie's young deputy friend.

Blushing furiously, she untied the apron and glared at him.

"Don't people knock on doors in this town? Or does having a badge give you the right to snoop?"

"I wasn't snooping. I knocked; you just didn't hear me over that racket on the stove... Are you going to let me in? I've come to see Frank."

"He's not back yet."

"Can I come in?"

"I guess so."

Mitch entered the kitchen, sat down, and looked around. "Where's Jessie?"

"She's in her room." Sara thought he was presumptuous, sitting down without being invited. Even though he was attractive, she wished he hadn't come by. Sort of.

"So how do you know Frank and Jessie?" he asked.

"You really are snooping, aren't you?" Sara folded her arms in front of her and decided she could be as rude as he was.

A loud *whoosh* exploded behind her and they both jumped and turned to the stove. The pressure cooker valve had blown, and peas were spewing up to the ceiling and falling all over the stovetop and counter.

"Oh, no! I've ruined it!" Sara cried as she hurriedly turned off the burner and grabbed dish towels to soak up the liquid mess. She glanced at Mitch and saw him staring helplessly. "Don't just sit there like a dolt. Help me get this cleaned up before Jessie sees it!"

"Too late," he said stoically, nodding toward the doorway. Sara closed her eyes for a moment before turning around. There was Jessie, eyes wide, looking at the ceiling and watching pea juice drip down to the pressure cooker, each drop making a tiny sizzle when it hit the hot lid.

Jessie put her hand over her mouth and turned away, her shoulders beginning to shake. Sara was devastated. This woman had been so kind to her and she'd made a huge mess in her kitchen. "I am so, so sorry! I'll clean it all up—really, I will."

Jessie's whole body was now shaking, and she turned to face Sara. Tears were running down her face and her silent convulsions erupted into laughter. She took one of the towels from Sara and began wiping the wall behind the stove. "Oh, honey, you don't know how badly I needed a laugh!"

***

Sara sat in the glider, stroking the ratty ball of gray fur in her lap.

"I see you've made a friend." Gracie narrowly opened her eyes at the sound of Frank's voice and raised her head. As he approached, the cat made a low guttural sound.

Sara looked quizzically at the man. "Did she just growl at you?" He sighed, took off his jacket, and folded it over the back of the chair. His shirt was limp, and sweat beaded across his forehead.

"That cat has never liked me."

Finally, a creature that doesn't worship the man, she thought. Aloud, she asked, "Why not?"

"I swatted at her once, years ago, and she's held a grudge ever since." He sat down wearily. "Where's Jessie?"

"She's in the back yard talking to someone from the Sheriff's Department. We saw him at the grocery store and he came by to see you."

Frank opened his mouth as though to say something, but stopped. He picked up his jacket again and pulled the newspaper clipping from a pocket. Sara sat quietly, then said, "She's really nice."

"Jessie? Yes, she is."

"There's something very, umm, comfortable about her. Know what I mean?"

"Yes. She and my brother were very happy together. In fact," he smiled, "they simply adored one another. Never were apart when they didn't have to be. Oh, they had their quarrels, some of them right sizeable, but they were happy. More than happy. They were content."

"Content is better than happy?"

"What I mean is, they were made for one another. They married and raised two nice, good children here. Loved this town, this house… each other. Never wanted any more than they had. Didn't see any reason to want more. They were living in their own paradise."

"Hmmm," muttered Sara, wondering if Frank felt the same contentment in his life. "Is that a generational thing?"

"Oh, partly, I guess, and partly because they were both from poor country families. They were living the life of Riley here."

Life of riley? Sara didn't know what that meant. Listening to old people was sometimes like hearing part of a conversation in a foreign language.

"Life isn't all that complicated," he went on. "We humans just make it that way."

Each fell silent to their own thoughts, him a bit curious at Sara's comments, and Sara a little embarrassed, wishing she could stop blurting out her feelings to this man. She needed his help, not his friendship.

"Oh, good, you're back. You have a visitor." Jessie came out on the porch, Mitch behind her. Frank rose and greeted him with a bear hug, both men talking at the same time. Gracie opened her eyes at the chatter, yawned, then put her head down again. *Content,* thought Sara. *Even the cat is content here.*

"Did you find out anything about your mysterious want ad?" Jessie asked.

Mitch looked curiously at Frank. "Are you coming out of retirement, Frank?"

"No, nothing like that. I saw something in the *New York Times* that caught my attention. Maybe you know something about it. I just asked Gary over at the newspaper office, and he thinks it's a misprint."

Frank handed him the newspaper clipping. Mitch read it and handed it back. "This was in the *New York Times*? It's got to be a mistake. There's no place like that anywhere in the county, and I've never heard of this person named in the ad. Gary's right. It has to be a misprint. Besides, why would a job in Deer Creek, Tennessee, be in a New York paper?"

"I guess you're right," Frank said. He looked at it again and set it aside, adding almost inaudibly, "Why *would* an ad about Deer Creek be in a New York paper?"

The men talked a few minutes more, and Mitch asked him to walk to his car with him. Sara moved from the glider so she could watch them without them seeing her. After a few minutes, Mitch pulled what looked like a folded envelope from his pocket and handed it to Frank, who shook his head and held up his hands in refusal. Mitch appeared to try to make him take it, then gave up and put it back in his pocket. He held out his hand and the men shook. The deputy left and Frank stood on the sidewalk a few minutes before going back to the house.

***

"Jessie, that was delicious. I swear, I don't know how you do it, but you can make the simplest meal seem like a king's banquet." Frank laid his fork and knife across his plate and leaned back, resting his hands on his full belly. The stewed potatoes, corn, peas, sliced tomatoes, and cornbread were all perfect. Although, he thought, the bowl of peas was oddly small.

***

The sheriff's patrol car circled the square slowly. Mitch knew he wasn't paying as much attention as he should be, but he wasn't worried. He'd been with the Sheriff's Department for over a year now and the town had not had a single burglary. There were drunken brawls, domestic calls, and the ubiquitous drug problems that no community escapes, no matter how small it is. But no break-ins. Patrolling the stores that circled the square was a waste of time.

He stopped for a red light and scanned the buildings around

him. Most were dark; some offered dim and feeble attempts at security lights inside. That's what made the fully lit shop across the intersection catch his eye. Lights were on in the unopened art gallery. He could see a man moving around and hanging pictures on the walls. That made sense. The opening was supposed to be in a few days, and the last time he'd looked in the window, the place wasn't close to being ready. He shook his head, wondering how quickly this business would go under. Why would anyone—especially two strangers with no apparent ties to this town—open an art gallery in Deer Creek? He didn't know much about business, and even less about art, but any fool could see this venture was doomed.

The light turned green, and Mitch slowly turned left to circle the square again. As he passed the gallery, he glanced over and saw two men walk into the store's front room, coming from the back storeroom. But there were no cars parked out front or anywhere close by. Curious, he drove to the next corner, turned, parked his cruiser, and got out. He cut across the darkened courthouse lawn toward the shop, unsure of what he had seen.

Not much goes unnoticed in such a small town. He'd heard around town that two men were setting up the gallery, and he hadn't heard of anyone being hired to help. He didn't think it could be a robbery—probably there wasn't even any money in the store yet—but he'd better be certain.

He stood in the darkness and watched. The first man he had seen put down the hammer. It looked like introductions were being made, followed with some gestures and talking. Mitch was too far away to see facial expressions or hear what was being said, but he got the vague impression that this wasn't a social call.

Their posture was stiff, almost confrontational. The third man was wearing a suit and his graying hair was pulled back in a pony-tail, reminding Mitch of a Steven Seagal movie character. When the suited stranger reached inside his jacket, Mitch almost expected him to pull out a gun. His own hand automatically moved to his holster. When the man withdrew a cell phone, Mitch let out his breath. He watched as the man pressed some buttons and held his phone to the other two, as if to show a message or picture. The man who'd had the hammer picked up a paper or envelope from the counter and all three went into the back. Mitch looked up and down the street, grateful that no one was there to see him spying in the dark. He sheepishly walked back to his car and drove off to finish his patrol.

He never saw the figure twenty feet behind him, watching from the shadows.

***

It was a pleasant night, surprisingly nice for June, so Mitch turned off the air conditioner and put down the windows. He thought about Frank. He wished he could have convinced him to take the money, but Mitch knew he never would. That man was a saint. God knows where he'd be now if Frank hadn't stepped in.

Mitch recalled those years. He had been hell on wheels in high school, giving his parents fits. He was never in trouble serious enough to land in jail, but he'd been close. He had hated Deer Creek, its small-town cliques, and everyone knowing everyone else's business. The day after high school graduation, he joined the Navy. He wanted to "see the world" and be as far from Deer Creek as he could get.

Five years later, he was back home, calmer and more mature, but still at loose ends. He met Frank through Jessie and Tony, of course. He remembered the night as if it were last week. Frank and his wife were in town for the weekend and the two couples and Mitch's parents were together for a cookout. Frank was having trouble with his car and Mitch had gotten roped into looking at it. He'd picked up a lot of mechanic's skills during his service years, and his folks were pushing him to look for a job as an auto mechanic.

While Mitch worked on the car, Frank started talking to him about his future—but he didn't talk like the others. He didn't give advice as much as he asked questions. He asked about his time in the service, the good ones, the bad ones, the people he admired, the ones he'd disliked, what he thought he'd gotten from the experience. It was Frank who suggested he go back to school, perhaps try the junior college nearby. *Don't be satisfied with just making a living,* he had said. *Make a life—one with some substance to it. Find out what the possibilities are for you. It's your one life. Make it meaningful.*

So he went to the junior college on a work scholarship that Frank helped him find. Unlike other students who worked in offices, Mitch was assigned duties in the maintenance department, fixing lawn mowers and anything else mechanical that needed repairs. Frank phoned him every couple of months, and even arranged for tutors when he struggled through hard classes and wanted to drop out. Then Mitch's dad became ill and bills started to mount. Frank talked him through that, too. It was Frank—not family or anyone from his own town—who quietly paid the funeral expenses when his father died. Frank convinced Mitch to tell his mother the money came from several back-paychecks that the Navy just happened to send him that month. Each time he saw him, he tried to repay the funeral costs. And each time, Frank refused to take it.

Frank was the best person he'd ever met. Someday, he would find a way to repay him.

4. TUESDAY

"He just walked right in? The nerve of that man!"

Jessie smiled with satisfaction. Karen's response was the reaction she'd wanted from her brother-in-law, who was too absorbed in that bizarre newspaper ad to understand how upset she had been by Saturday's incident.

"Why, that's trespassing at the very least. Let's call Mitch and see if he can arrest him, or give him a ticket, or, *or something*. Did he push you aside when he came in the door? That would be assault for sure." Karen was indignant on behalf of her friend, and her imagination had already moved into overdrive. She and Jessie were prolific readers of mystery novels that they exchanged each month, books full of cold killers who boldly shoved their way into homes of innocent victims. To top it off, she'd heard plenty of cop stories from her deputy son.

"No, no, he didn't actually push me, and I was holding the door open, so technically he wasn't trespassing. He didn't do anything illegal." Jessie gave a little shudder. "He just made me feel, well, very uncomfortable… But he certainly liked Anthony's pictures.

At least he has good taste." She shrugged her shoulders and put her purse in the middle drawer of the filing cabinet where the women volunteers stashed their handbags. Her dislike of the man had not lessened, but she didn't want to worry Karen. "So, anything new today?"

The women put aside their private chatter and Karen gave her a quick update on the roster of current patients—five at the moment and a new one, a dementia patient, being transferred in this afternoon.

What was once a run-down old house two blocks off the square had been leased by the regional hospital a few years ago and converted into a three-patient hospice as part of a short training program. Karen's husband was one of those patients. Well before the program ended, the county, the hospital board, and the town of Deer Creek realized the value of residential hospice. It was a logical solution to an acute dilemma. Like in so many other rural areas, the county's population was aging rapidly. Many residents moved to more urban areas where they could readily find employment, often leaving their parents without day-to-day family support. The terminally-ill needed care. When insurance payments were exhausted, hospitals couldn't and wouldn't keep these patients. Families desperately needed help.

Frequently, the ill were elderly who either lived alone or lived with a spouse—also elderly—who was physically exhausted after months of care-giving. Not that hospice care was cheap. While nursing care typically was covered by Medicare and most insurance companies, the cost of room and board at a residential hospice like Deer Creek's ran to hotel rates and usually was not covered by insurance.

The county and the town of Deer Creek scrimped together enough to buy the house and remodel two more rooms for patients. The vacant lot behind it was donated for an addition, and private donations, mostly from the "old money" families in town, allowed the facility to grow. Then some serious money was donated anonymously, and now Community Hospice was a small but model facility that quietly (very quietly) paid the bills for those patients who couldn't pay anything.

There were presently rooms for seven patients. Upstairs in the original house, the rooms had been converted to the director's office, a conference room, a staff lounge, and restroom. The downstairs housed the lobby area, a family room, a tiny chapel, two restrooms, and a kitchen.

In the lobby, Jessie set out a carafe of fresh coffee and a box of pastries dropped off that morning by someone from a local church, then began her rounds to the patients. As a volunteer, she routinely sat with patients who wanted company, read to them, helped feed the ones who could swallow, arranged flowers or books—whatever was needed in the few hours she was there.

All the patient rooms were in the new part of the building—a bright and airy addition that flowed seamlessly from the rear of the house. The nurse's station began where the original back porch had stood. Around and behind it was a spacious hallway lined with seven doors. Jessie stopped at the desk and greeted the two staff members on duty, Alice, the R.N., and Gerald, the nurse's aide.

"Miss Jessie, what are you doing here?" asked Alice, surprised. "You were just here yesterday."

"I took Annie's shift. You wouldn't want her here today, believe me. She's sneezing her head off. Can I do anything for you two?"

"Could you find a short vase for these flowers? I've looked but can't find anything the right size." Gerald handed her a plastic grocery bag with a handful of wilting impatiens wrapped loosely in a wet paper towel. "Oops, these seem to have come with a couple of ladybugs," he added. "Mr. Yarbrough just brought them in. What a sweet man. He brings Mrs. Yarbrough flowers every morning—and such a variety. I've driven by their house for years and never saw one flower out front. They must have a lot of flowerbeds in their back yard. Just goes to show, you never know about people."

"Yes, you never know," she replied. "I'll fix them up and take them in to her. How's Mr. Foley?"

"He's asleep now," said Alice quietly. "He had a rough night." John Foley was 61 and had lung cancer. Unlike the other patients, he received hospice care at home and was here now to give his wife a break. Community Hospice allowed respite care for five days a month. Based on his increased pain and other changes he was experiencing, Alice didn't think Mr. Foley would be going home again.

Alice Stanley had been a part of the staff almost from the start. After visiting the facility when it was still a training program, she couldn't shake it from her thoughts. With 30-plus years as a floor nurse, she was burned out by her hospital job. Mainly she was tired of the bureaucracy, the long hours, erratic shifts, overbearing personalities—all the typical negatives faced by working men and women. Here at the hospice, there were still long hours and occasional conflicts, and just the nature of the business meant there was stress. But here she felt she had found her true calling. She was professional, calm and kind with her patients. But she could be curt and intolerant with family members whom she believed were either overly demanding or under responsive to their dying relative. Those who fell in between, she treated respectfully.

Alice expertly dealt with her patients' needs and fears, as well as those of their families. Because patients were usually on unfathomable amounts of painkillers, she frequently had to assure family members that their loved ones wouldn't become addicted because the drugs were so badly needed to control the pain. She could never understand their worry over addiction. What would it matter anyway if the person was only going to live another three weeks and the drugs made that time tolerable?

While she might occasionally be sharp with family members, she was generous with praise for the volunteers who donated a few hours each week. Most gave their time after having lost someone in hospice care. To ensure their offer wasn't just a reactionary gesture, they had to wait at least one year before they were allowed to participate; only then could they attend the intensive training program required. Alice was especially fond of Jessie, who seemed to have a gift for comforting people.

It was a busy morning for the staff and volunteers. Of the five patients, three were bedridden. Hazel Yarbrough had her doting husband with her. John Foley was finally asleep. And Geraldine Mason was letting Jessie read a detective novel aloud to her. In her early nineties, Geraldine actually preferred steamy love stories, but that was something she'd just as soon her visiting fellow church members not know. There weren't many choices one could make about dying, Geraldine told herself. Taking a juicy little secret to the grave was a choice she quite enjoyed.

Family members were visiting the other two residents: Norman Rosencrans, who was somewhat mobile and could get himself in and out of a wheelchair, and Albert Perry, the sole "walkie-talkie" resident, who insisted on wearing his Sunday church clothes and spent his time sitting quietly in the outside gardens. He had been here a week, and anyone seeing him outside joking with his grandchildren would have mistaken him for a visitor. Up close, though, one could see the toll his heart disease was taking.

"Jessie, it's time to go," said Karen from the doorway. "I'll wait for you outside." Jessie nodded and finished the page before marking the book and putting it on the nightstand. "Miss Geraldine, I'll be back soon. I hope you have a good day now." She took the old woman's cold hand between hers and held it briefly.

"Thank you, Jess," the frail woman said, her voice weak. "I don't know if I'll see you next time. I came here to die, and I need to get on with it. I'm not afraid, so don't you fret about me." Geraldine closed her eyes and dozed off, drained by the effort of conversation.

Minutes later, Jessie met Karen at her car. "I swear, the hours fly by when I'm here." Karen agreed, then suggested they stop for coffee before going home to their empty houses. All of a sudden, Jessie groaned. "Oh, no. I meant to call Francis after I got here." Seeing Karen's puzzled look, she explained. "Francis came in yesterday and spent the night—he and a young woman. I forgot to tell you this morning because I was telling you about that Roberts man. I left before they woke up, and I meant to call after I got here to let him know where I was and when I'd be back."

Karen's eyes got huge and her mouth dropped open. "Frank brought a woman to your house? A *young* woman? What is he thinking?"

"Oh, Karen, it's nothing like that. I really haven't had a chance to ask him about her, but I think she's a new 'cause.' You know how Francis is, always bringing home a lost dog. Not literally, of course. He prefers cats I'm sure. And this girl is quite lovely... and seems rather smart. She's just a bit unusual, a little rough around the edges. And to tell you the truth, I'm not real fond of that blue hair or the piercings. But I don't think she's in any trouble."

Karen stared at her friend. Jessie could go on and on and sometimes didn't make much sense. But she was truly one in a million. Karen had never had a close friend before Jessie. She had been married forever, it seemed, raised four children, and then just when she and Hank thought things were about to get easier for them, along came Mitch. None of their children were planned, but Mitch was definitely an accident. Busy with her large family, Karen never made the time to cultivate deep friendships among her women acquaintances. Until one day, she was summoned to pick up Mitch from the principal's office. Karen was distraught, and it was Jessie, the school secretary, who calmed her, reassured her that her son wasn't a hoodlum, and told her that she was close to a couple of his teachers and would ask them to look out for him. After that, Mitch was in trouble less and his grades improved. Whether it was Jessie's intervention or just coincidence, Karen never knew. What she did know was from that day forward, they gradually became the closest of friends.

Now she gave Jessie a quick hug. "We'll get together later. Tell Frank hi for me."

***

Frank looked dreadful. He was pale and was nervously tapping his foot on the floor. Sara sat at the opposite end of the kitchen table, eating a bowl of cereal and watching Frank warily.

"I am so, so sorry," Jessie apologized. "I forgot to leave you a note this morning, and then I was going to call you from hospice, but I got busy and it just slipped my mind." Jessie put her purse and keys on the counter and looked closely at her brother-in-law. "Francis, are you feeling well? Surely you weren't worried about me not being here."

Frank looked at her with a pained expression. "No, I thought you might be there. It's Bill, my friend who owns the diner. Mary called me just a few minutes ago. He had a heart attack last night."

Jessie dropped to a chair. She had never met Bill, but she had heard Frank speak of him so often that she felt as though she had known him for years. "Is he...?"

"He's stable. Mary didn't know anything more. Or at least she didn't tell me anything more. I told her I would come back. I can stay with him while she's at the diner. They can't afford to close it, even for a few days. Funny, I woke up today thinking about him. In fact, I walked over to the gallery this morning, when I realized you weren't here and saw that your car was gone. I figured you were working. So I went over and asked if they might be interested in displaying some of Bill's wooden boxes. I thought it might be an opportunity for him."

Frank frowned. He had stopped tapping his foot and was now repeatedly smoothing out the folds of a paper napkin on the table, one of his little habits that Jessie had seen before. "You met those men at the art gallery?" she asked.

"Just one. A guy named Roberts. He said to bring them by and he'd look at them. But he didn't seem to know much about woodworking as art. As a matter of fact, he didn't seem interested in talking to me at all until I told him I was staying here with you. Then he got real interested. Asked me questions about Tony's paintings." The color had come back into Frank's face and, as he talked, his demeanor changed. "Jessie, there's something odd about that man. I understand now what you meant. I didn't like him at all." He picked up his coffee cup, then put it down again, his mind bouncing back to his sick friend. "I have to go back right away. You understand, don't you?"

Jessie nodded. Francis was being somewhat solicitous, she thought, but for a change she rather liked it. That Roberts man coming into her house had unnerved her, and, quite truthfully, she wanted Francis to stay.

"I guess I'd better get my things if we're going back now."

Jessie and Frank looked over at Sara. Deep in thought, they had forgotten she was there. The girl rose, put her bowl in the sink, and silently left the kitchen.

Things weren't going as Frank had expected. It had been three days since he met Sara and he didn't know what to do with her. He felt sure he could figure out something, but he was distracted. He didn't want to leave Jessie just yet. She seemed uneasy. And rightly so with that questionable character living just beyond her back door. Then there was that peculiar newspaper ad nagging at his brain. And Bill. There was no doubt he needed to go see about Bill. If only he could just stop time for a few days, put one situation on hold while he dealt with another.

"Don't worry about us," Jessie said. Frank turned to look at her, startled. Had he been talking out loud without realizing it? *Again.* Or was she reading his mind?

"Of course you need to go, right away... but why don't you leave Sara with me for a few days, then come back this weekend?"

"Oh, Jessie, I can't let you do that." He lowered his voice. "I just met the girl last weekend. Now I'm sure she's a nice young lady, it's just that..." He stopped, not knowing how to finish.

"SARA," Jessie called out, ignoring him. "Can you come here for a minute?" A few seconds later, Sara walked into the kitchen, backpack slung over her shoulder.

"How would you like to stay here with me for the rest of the week? Francis can come back for you Saturday or Sunday. He's going to be awfully busy for a few days, and I could use some help around here. It's high time this house had a good spring cleaning, even though it's already summer, and I'm just not up to it. It seems all I do is give it a hit and a lick and then I'm worn out. I'll pay you, of course. A hundred dollars." Glancing up at the dingy kitchen curtains and the dusty knick-knacks on the window sill, she changed her offer. "No, that won't be enough. How about two-hundred?"

That was not at all what Sara was expecting—or Frank. Sara put down her backpack. Two-hundred dollars would get her home. Maybe she could even get home before her dad got back. He'd never have to know she'd left. Frank wasn't objecting, and she liked the idea of hanging out here for a few days. Besides, she didn't mind housework, especially getting paid for it. She smiled broadly at Jessie. "Where do I start?"

5. WEDNESDAY

Sara's muscles ached. Yesterday she had cleaned the bedrooms and bathrooms from top to bottom, pulling furniture away from the walls and cleaning the cobwebs and dust behind them. She'd scrubbed the bathroom tile and washed the shower curtains. She and Jessie had turned mattresses and taken down, washed, and ironed the bedroom curtains. This morning, she cleaned the living room and what she was now calling the "art" room. Neither took long since those rooms were so sparsely furnished. In fact, other than the kitchen and Jessie's bedroom, the house was devoid of clutter and tchotchkes—or doodads, as Jessie called them.

Now she rummaged through kitchen cabinets, finally finding something to wash windows: a plain plastic spray bottle with the words "glass cleaner" handwritten on a plain white label. Sara unscrewed the top and sniffed. It smelled like vinegar. The bottles she'd found in the bathroom were similar. She smiled, both surprised and impressed at Jessie's home-made, environment-friendly cleaners.

Although her back was complaining, Sara found the physical

work revitalizing. Each completed task, no matter how insignificant, gave her a feeling of accomplishment. Jessie *ooh*ed and *aah*ed over every cleaned surface and her appreciation made Sara want to do the next chore even better. If she didn't need the money to get home, she would have done this for free. The work helped her to stop thinking about the recent mistakes she had made. Besides, she liked being here, and she liked this odd woman who treated her so kindly.

"Goodness gracious, girl, you've got to pace yourself. You're going to wear yourself out." Jessie motioned for her to sit down while she pulled a pitcher of tea from the refrigerator. "The house looks great. It smells so fresh and clean, and it just feels good, knowing there aren't dust-bunnies under my furniture." She looked around with delight. "Tomorrow we'll do the kitchen."

Sara suppressed a smile, knowing the "we" was in name only. Although her host made an effort to participate, she lacked the strength for some chores and took frequent breaks. She looked around the room, taking inventory of the next day's tasks. Gesturing toward a note taped to the clock on the wall, she said, "Jessie, I don't mean to be nosy, but what does '+1' mean?"

"Oh, that's just my reminder for Daylight Saving Time."

"Uh, would you like me to change the clock for you?"

"No need for that. I'll take down the note in October." Jessie poured two glasses of tea and put them on the table, then turned to get a package of cookies from the cabinet. "I can't remember when the house was last this clean," she said, smiling warmly at Sara. "Do you like grapes?" she suddenly asked.

"Sure."

"Then walk outside to the fence on the left. There's a trellis with a grapevine. Pick us a handful. You'll be able to tell which are ripe."

A few minutes later, Sara was back, cupping her hands against her midriff to avoid spilling the purple grapes.

"Oh, those look good," said Jessie, holding a bowl under Sara's hands to catch them. They tumbled into the bowl and she set it on the kitchen table.

"Aren't you going to wash them?" Sara asked.

"No need. I never use pesticides." She picked up a grape, and in a quick motion, kissed it, held it up in the air in front of her, and said, "Just kiss it up to God."

Sara recoiled as though she had been struck. Her face was pale and looked as though she might faint. Jessie was dumbfounded. "What is it? What's wrong?" The girl was looking at her strangely, her eyes filling with tears. Two teardrops escaped and ran down her cheeks, leaving a slight trail of black mascara.

"Sara, tell me what's wrong. Were you stung? Did a spider bite you?"

"What you said…"

"What are you talking about? Pesticides?"

"No. *Kiss it…*" Her words were a whisper.

"Kiss it up to God? That's just an expression. Like the five-second rule when something lands on the floor. You pick it up quickly and it doesn't have to be washed. Or you 'kiss' it and trust that God protects you from germs." Her explanation sounded silly even as she said it, but Jessie would have spouted nursery rhymes if it would calm Sara.

"I know what it means," the girl said quietly. "My mother used to say that."

Jessie put her arm around Sara and guided her to a chair and then sat down across from her. Sara put her hands around the white china bowl that now held the grapes, looking at them and not at the woman. "My mother died when I was six. Sometimes I don't think of her at all. Then all of a sudden, something reminds me of her and it's as if she's in the room. It's kind of a shock, that's all."

The older woman placed her wrinkled hands on top of Sara's, still gripping the bowl. She'd had that bowl since the day she got married. *Back then, it gleamed, smooth and shiny and bright as the future. Now it's covered with tiny cracks, so many you'd think it would shatter at the slightest touch. People are like that,* Jessie thought. *Lives get filled with cracks. Some break. Others keep going, held together with unseen strength. Which one is Sara?*

"I'm sorry," the older woman said simply. "That must have been very hard for you, to lose her when you were so young." They sat quietly for a few minutes. Jessie didn't pry, and Sara revealed nothing more. Gradually they drank their tea, ate the cookies and grapes, and returned to an impersonal conversation, discussing the grapes, their tea break, and how many cleaning chores were left. Jessie spoke easily. Age and experience had taught her patience; if Sara wanted to talk more about herself, she would. Meanwhile, if she couldn't comfort the girl, she would simply make her comfortable. Strange how two words could be so alike and so different, Jessie thought. So she chattered away, not stopping until she saw the girl's countenance relax.

It was good to have a young face in the house, she realized. Jessie missed her children. Maybe she would start visiting them more, maybe stay with them for a little while—not long, just a few days at a time. It would be good to get away, she thought. She involuntarily looked out the window, across her back yard, across the alley, to the rear of the shop now housing the new gallery. Her smile faded. Yes, it would be very good to get away.

Sara looked outside to see what might have caught Jessie's attention, and saw only the yard and building behind it. Remembering how upset the woman had been about the gallery owner stopping by, she asked, "Are you afraid of that man?"

"Afraid?" Jessie looked at her young companion in surprise. Was she afraid? If so, of what? Deer Creek's newest resident, Burton Roberts, had come into her house—sort of uninvited—and admired the artwork on her walls. That was all. Hadn't she said as much to Karen when she described it to her? She didn't understand why the incident bothered her so. He had been a little discourteous to her at the gallery, but was polite to bring the forgotten bag of books to her house. True, he was somewhat rude to come in without being asked, but it was only because he was drawn in by Anthony's paintings, and maybe even said so. She didn't exactly remember. What was wrong with that? She shook her head and tried to assuage her concern. "No, I'm not afraid, just puzzled. But it's nothing to worry your pretty head about."

Sara couldn't help herself. She laughed out loud. "You're funny," she said, her own sadness dispelled by her growing affection for this woman. "First you call me a rainbow, now I've got a pretty head. So the blue hair and nose ring and tattoo don't bother you?"

It was Jessie's turn to laugh. "Honey, I used to work in a high school. I've seen it all. No, it doesn't bother me... well, except for the tattoo," she admitted. "The rest will come off when you're tired of them. It's no different than ratted hair or frosted lipstick or mini-skirts. Every generation has its own thing."

With a puzzled look toward the blue bangs, she asked, "How do you get it that color?"

Sara wrapped a strand of blue around her finger. "Powdered bleach mixed with developer to take the color out, then just dye it blue. It only lasts a little while, then the roots start to show."

"Well, I'll be." Jessie shook her head, then pointed to Sara's hand with the blue painted nails. "It's just as well that you didn't finish your manicure. By the time you're through with the cleaning, this will be all chipped off."

Sara grinned again, enjoying Jessie's candor. "I'll tell you a secret," she said, turning her wrist so the intricately drawn reddish-brown sun was looking at Jessie. "The tattoo isn't real. It's just henna and it'll wear off. But let's don't tell Frank yet. He stares at it when he thinks I don't see. I can tell he doesn't approve, but he's too nice to say anything."

***

"This sucks. I'm not going to stand around and let these hicks laugh at me. You can have your little party by yourself." Harris had just returned from the hardware store with a can of turpentine. He looked around the soon-to-open gallery with disdain, gave Burton a disgusted look, and stomped through the shop and curtained doorway. Burton heard him go up the stairs, then come back down and leave through the back door. Before he realized what was happening, he heard the car—his car—drive away. He knew he wouldn't see him for hours, and maybe not until after tomorrow's opening.

Just as well. He'd probably say something stupid—or worse, show up high. He's going to get us jammed up if I don't watch it. After this deal is over, I'm going solo. I needed him in New Orleans, and I need him now. But after he's finished upstairs, he can go his own way. He's too hot-headed and unpredictable.

Burton spent the next hour hanging a few more pieces and setting up for the opening. He didn't expect to make any sales, but he had to make it look authentic. He set a neatly printed sign on the counter: *Cash or Checks Only*. That wasn't customary, he knew, but he had to keep things as simple as possible. Credit cards were an unnecessary complication. He couldn't put off opening the gallery any longer without drawing attention. Once it was open and the curiosity seekers came and went, he didn't expect many customers. He could sit back, blend into the town, and get on with business. If last night's meeting was indicative of what was in store, he'd be out of here soon enough.

He assessed the room. The lighting here wasn't the best, but he'd made it work. All those months working in galleries in L.A. and New Orleans had taught him how to display artwork, how to appraise it, and how to sell ridiculously expensive paintings and sculptures to people who bought them because someone told them the artist was the next Andy Warhol. He hated the rich who collected art for investments. They had no true love for art, they had no taste. He, on the other hand, had taste. Unfortunately, he had expensive taste. Way too expensive for a living made as a gallery assistant, or even a gallery owner. He shrugged and went to the back, where he picked up his cell and started searching through his email.

***

Hot and tired, Sara tucked her hair behind her ears and surveyed the last window. She was pleased with her work and went inside to find Jessie. She found her in the living room, just hanging up the phone. The woman's shoulders were slumped and her eyes were wet. "That was Karen," she said. "We lost one of our patients today. Mr. Foley passed away." She rubbed her eyes and straightened. "I don't know why it always catches me off guard. But it does."

"If it bothers you so much, why do you go there?" asked Sara. "It must be so depressing."

"Oh, no, dear, it's not depressing," Jessie answered, shaking her head. "It makes me feel good. Not to see people die, of course, but to know that I'm helping them in their last weeks or days. It is hard, but saying goodbye is a part of life; the only way to avoid it is to never say hello. Then think of all the love and happiness you'd miss."

She sighed. "I'm probably not explaining this very well. I don't think of hospice as a place where people go to die, but rather as a refuge for very sick people at the end of their lives. It's not like a hospital, although of course we have a doctor and a nurse. The patients get pain relief, but they don't get medical treatment. They're being sheltered and comforted and helped to rest. So much of the time, that's what they need and what their families need. Simply rest."

"Like a nursing home?"

"Oh, no, very different from a nursing home." The doorbell interrupted them, and Jessie jumped at the noise. Seeing Jessie hesitate, Sara went to the door and opened it. There stood Mitch.

"Hi," he said.

"What do you want?"

Mitch feigned shock. "Is that any way to address an officer of the law?"

"Who is it?" Jessie said in the background, then making her way to the door, said, "Oh, it's Mitchell! Come in, come in."

Sara backed away and the officer walked in, warmly hugging Jessie while giving Sara a playful smirk.

"I was in the neighborhood and just got off duty. Thought I'd check on you. I see you still have company. Frank's still here?"

"Francis had to go back for a few days. And what do you mean, you were in the neighborhood? You're never on my street."

Mitch grinned and shook his head. "It was Mrs. Ferguson again. Another funeral. This time it was a mass. She never misses a funeral mass. The wine, you know. Father Roger called and asked me to come get her and take her home." Looking at Sara, he explained, "Mrs. Ferguson lives a few houses down the street. Whenever she hears there's a funeral in town, she wanders in. Most people don't mind. But sometimes it's a problem, like when she shows up at the funeral of a man whose family hardly knows her. The family starts thinking she's an old lover or something." He rolled his eyes. "It's either this or someone stealing flowers. One day the sheriff is going to realize he doesn't need any deputies … So, you doing okay, Jessie?"

"Fine, just fine. Sara, bless her heart, has cleaned my house from top to bottom. And all that work has worn me out. I think I need a nap." She smiled slyly at Mitch. "And Sara probably would love to get out of this house for a little while. She's been cooped up here for two days. Why don't you show her around town?"

Sara wanted to crawl under the floor, she was so embarrassed. "That's a great idea," Mitch said, amused at Sara's discomfort.

"I-I don't know," Sara said. "I'm a mess and I don't have any clean clothes to change into. Maybe some other time."

"Nonsense," the older woman said. "Just pull something out of the closet in your room. I'm sure there's something in there that will fit you. Mitchell, come in the kitchen with me. I want to tell you about Mr. Foley."

Before Sara could protest again, the two walked to the back of the house, leaving Sara frustrated and a little annoyed. Well, why not, she told herself. While Jessie led Mitch to the kitchen, she went down the hallway to the little bedroom and attached bathroom.

She took one look in the mirror and groaned. The windows and the rest of the house might be clean, but she certainly was not. Her tee-shirt and jeans were dirtier than she'd thought, and wiping the sweat off her face had done a number on the mascara she put on this morning. She wondered about Mitch. Did he really want to drive her around town, or was he just placating Jessie? She looked into the face staring back at her. *Who cares what he really thinks? Alex is gone. I'm here and I'm moving on, too. I've got to start somewhere. It may as well be here and now.*

Sara stripped off her clothes and piled them in the corner. When she got back in an hour or so, she would ask Jessie if she could use her washer and dryer. She rinsed off quickly in the shower, not even waiting for the water to get warm, wrapped a towel around her body, and went to the bedroom.

Although Jessie hadn't said so, it was clear that the room she was staying in had been Jessie's daughter's. Although not "girly," it held a few remnants of a teenage girl's room. Hoping there would be something passable that she could wear for the afternoon, she opened the closet. She had seen the long garment bag the first night she was there—and the three or four pairs of shoes lined up on the closet floor, each carefully dust-proofed by a plastic shower cap. Another of Jessie's quirky household inventions. She slowly unzipped the plastic behemoth, recalling a similar bag hanging in her dad's closet. Sara used to open it when he wasn't around, her hands touching each item while her mind tried desperately to remember how her mother looked wearing it. She could never remember.

She shook off the memory and thumbed through the hangers. There were shirts, jeans, and a few dresses. She looked at the jeans and was surprised to see that she could probably wear some of them. The tops were plain, either white button-up shirts or solid colored tee-shirts. Curious, she pulled out a couple of dresses and tried them on.

Sara wondered what Jessie's daughter was like and how she fared growing up in this small town. How lucky she was to have Jessie for a mother. Or did they argue?

She put aside her thoughts and concentrated on the clothes. She'd wear the blue dress. It would be cool, and she liked how she looked in it. That would give that hotshot deputy something to think about. On the other hand, she didn't want him to think that she was trying to impress him. Just to be sure, she put on her flip-flops.

Sara glanced at herself in the dresser mirror, took a deep breath, and went out to face Jessie and Mitch. In the living room, she found Jessie alone, sitting on the couch and brushing Gracie. Mitch was nowhere in sight. Sara looked around angrily. "He changed his mind and left?" she asked tersely.

"He'll be back any minute," Jessie said quickly. From the bits and pieces that Francis had told her, she knew that Sara's boyfriend had abruptly abandoned her in Knoxville. Then Francis left her here, and now Sara must think that Mitchell was doing the same. Oh dear, she thought, she should have anticipated this. Well, since this was her idea, she'd better get Sara calmed down before Mitchell got back. Poor child, she probably thinks people have been leaving her ever since her mother died.

"He had to take the squad car back and get his own car." She smiled broadly at Sara. "You look beautiful."

Now Sara was embarrassed. This was too much. Her emotions had been all over the board today. It was exhausting. The last thing she wanted to do right now was go out with a stranger. She wanted to go home. Or stay here with Jessie. She didn't know what she wanted.

Jessie was babbling on. "As you probably guessed, that dress was my daughter's. I think Elizabeth wore it in high school and college. I always loved the colors in it. It really fits you well." Jessie scooted Gracie off her lap and brushed the cat hair off her pants. "You look pretty in blue," she said. "And it goes with your hair."

Sleeveless and scooped-neck, the garment was a faded blue cotton dress. The top was covered with multi-colored embroidery with tiny mirror-like decorations scattered throughout. The dress hung loosely around Sara's narrow waist, where the blue changed into tie-dyed colors of red and orange, and then fell into blue fringe at her knees.

"Yes, that's a good choice," Jessie continued, "especially in this heat." A rap on the door signaled that Mitch was back. Jessie let him in. Not only had he switched cars, but he had also changed clothes, trading his uniform for a white polo, cutoffs, and loafers with no socks. Jessie thought he looked quite handsome. Sara thought he looked like a Ralph Lauren ad—definitely not her type.

"Jessie, Mom said she'd call you in a bit. Here, she sent you one of her latest creations—but I wouldn't eat it if I were you. She's trying out a new recipe. It's for another contest she's entering." He handed Jessie a glass bowl with a plastic lid, and looked at Sara, surprised but pleased that she'd put on a dress to go out with him. "Ready to see the big town of Deer Creek?"

"You kids have a good time. Take your time." Jessie shooed them out, and watched from the window as they walked to the curb. Once they were at the car, she locked the front door, and then carried the bowl to the back of the house. Glancing out the back window, she stopped and bolted the kitchen door, too.

Mitch looked sideways at Sara, who was studying him curiously. "What?" he asked.

"Do you live with your mother?"

"Yep."

"How old are you?"

"Do you mean, aren't I a little old to be living with my mother?"

"Just curious."

"Okay, Miss Curiosity. I'm 31. What else do you want to know about me?"

"Do you like living here?"

He looked surprised. That wasn't the question he expected. He thought for a moment, then answered, "Yes, I guess I do. Next question?"

"Where are we going and how long will we be gone?"

"You're rather direct, aren't you?" By this time, they had gone half-way around the town square. Mitch found an empty parking space and swung in. "To tell you the truth, there's probably not much in Deer Creek that would interest you. So we're going to walk across the square, I'm going to buy us a burger and a milkshake, and then I'll take you back to Jessie's. Unless," he said, giving her a more serious look, "you tell me you really would like me to show you around." He put the car in park and turned off the ignition. Sara sat quietly, her hand on the door handle.

"I'm sorry. I didn't mean to sound rude."

"Okay. No offense taken. I'm hungry. How about you? Or has Jessie been feeding you non-stop?"

"Actually," said Sara, opening the door, "I think she forgot about lunch. A milkshake sounds great."

They went in. It was mid-afternoon, and they were the only customers in the restaurant. The waitress behind the counter smiled at them, filled two glasses with water, and carried them and a single menu to the table where the pair sat. Turning to Sara, she said, "We're out of lemonade, but you can order anything else."

Sara ordered an egg salad sandwich and chocolate milkshake, then held the menu out to Mitch.

The waitress laughed, and took the menu out of Sara's hand. "Cheeseburger and banana milkshake. Same thing every day as long as I've worked here. The man is totally predictable."

Sara hadn't realized how hungry she was, and since Mitch had offered to pay, she was determined to be pleasant. It wasn't as hard as she thought, since he didn't ask any personal questions, he wasn't bad looking, and he was interesting, too. He talked easily, and that put her at ease.

"You should try the banana shake," he said, spooning out a scoop and offering it to her.

"No thanks, I don't taste other people's food."

"Your loss." He shrugged and swallowed the bite, then looked at her quizzically. "You never told me—how long have you known Frank?"

Sara thought for a moment, then said simply, "Sunday."

At first Mitch didn't get it, thinking she had misunderstood his question. He was about to ask again when he saw the amusement in her eyes. "This is Wednesday."

"I know what day it is."

"You're saying that you met Frank on Sunday… of this week?"

"Yes." She waited for him to ask more, but he didn't. He just looked at her for the longest time, wondering, but not asking.

Sara wondered, too, but her wonder—and gratitude—was that Frank had not told his friends how they had met. She smiled. Sunday seemed like weeks ago. "He's been very nice. At times, I think he's a simple, gentle man," she said. "Then other times I think he's much more complex."

"What do you mean?"

"Oh, I don't know. It's like he's not telling all he knows. And he's mysterious about all the phone calls he gets."

Mitch was perplexed, and also uncomfortable with her words. Frank was his hero. "I wouldn't call him simple, maybe just straightforward, down-to-earth. He's an incredible person. One of the best I've ever known."

"But don't you ever feel that there's something going on that he doesn't talk about? For example, when I first saw him, it was in a diner, kind of like this place. And different people were making a fuss over him. It seemed as if none of them knew each other, but they all knew Frank." She paused, realizing that she was unable to convey the oddness that she had seen. She changed the subject to Jessie and soon had Mitch talking about his high school days and knowing Jessie from the times he was sent to the principal's office.

"She's a gem," he said. "She was great to me back then, and now that she and Mom are close, it seems like she's part of my family. Sometimes she's a little unusual, but in good ways."

Sara didn't contradict him. Jessie was a little different, admittedly, but she was nice. Better than nice. She was genuine. There wasn't an ounce of pretense in her and Sara loved that about her. She thought Mitch might be wrong about Frank—not that he wasn't a good person, but she was sure he had things going on in his life that he didn't share with his friends in Deer Creek.

As the pair ate, Mitch thought he could talk forever to her, just to have those intense eyes look back at him. They hardly left his face, as though every word he said was important to her. He recalled how she was completely focused on the little girl in the grocery store. That was what had caught his attention: her intensity and her eyes, charged with sincerity.

"Why are you looking like that?"

"Like what?"

"Like you have a secret or something."

He shrugged. "Nothing, just thinking."

When they were through with their sandwiches, they poured their half-finished milkshakes into take-out cups and headed back to the car. As they crossed the street, a horn beeped several times. A pretty blonde in a red convertible waved at Mitch. Her face darkened when she saw Sara, and she sped away.

"Someone special?" Sara asked.

"Nope."

Sara started to tease him about the girl, but a figure across the street caught her attention. A man was repeatedly opening and closing a door, then disappeared inside. There was an empty art easel in the picture window. "Is that the new gallery that Jessie was talking about?"

"Yeah, it's supposed to open tomorrow. I imagine Jessie will be there a lot, with her being so interested in art."

"Oh, I don't think so," Sara answered. "Didn't your mother tell you what happened?" The confused look he gave her said she had not, so Sara told him the brief story. "That's why Frank came here Monday," she concluded. "He said she sounded weird on the phone and he was worried about her."

This was all news to Mitch. "Let's walk over and look inside."

***

"There, that should help." The shop owner jiggled the bell on the door and frowned. *The isolation is getting to me. Now I'm talking to myself. Damn that Harris. He'd better start doing his share of the work around here. Like this bell. I told him last week to put a bell on the door so we wouldn't be caught off-guard when people walked in. It's getting so I have to do everything myself.*

He was walking to the back room when he heard the bell ring. He swung around, realizing too late that he had left the door unlocked. He took in the couple. Rubes, he thought to himself. None of his L.A. customers would ever have come into a gallery carrying drinks in Styrofoam cups.

"I'm sorry, we're not open yet." He gave his best apologetic smile and said, "We open tomorrow."

"No problem. We'll come back," Mitch said, then as if he just remembered, he looked at Sara. "Oh, didn't you say Jessie thought one of her books fell out of her bag in here?" Before Sara could say anything, Mitch looked back at the man. "Maybe you're the person who returned some books to our neighbor? She said she thought one of the books might have fallen out and still be here. Did you happen to run across a paperback?" He made a pretense of looking about the floor, as if the book would suddenly spring from its hiding place.

"No, I'm sure it isn't here. You said you're a neighbor of hers?"

"Yeah, she and my mom are good friends."

Burton saw an opportunity. "Yes, I'm the one who returned her bag. I couldn't help but noticing when I was there that day that she had some intriguing artwork. I was thinking of showcasing some of the local art, perhaps featuring a local artist occasionally here in the gallery. Maybe you could convince her to loan out two or three paintings?"

"Sure, I'll be happy to try," Mitch said amiably. "Do you have a card or something with a phone number on it? I'll talk to her—or better yet, I'll ask my mom to talk to her."

Burton walked to the counter as if to get a card, and Mitch followed. The young man moved to the end of the counter opposite the shopkeeper and lazily leaned against it, looking around the room and giving Sara his most charming smile.

"Our cards haven't come from the printer yet," Burton said, lying easily. "I'm sure I have something in the back I can put my number on for you to give her. I'll be right back." He walked behind the counter and through the curtained doorway. As soon as the curtains closed Mitch peeked behind the counter. The shelf behind and under it was nearly as empty as the countertop. No flyers, no receipt book, no credit card machine, no cash box, not even a pen or pencil. Just an unwashed coffee cup, a cell phone, and part of a folded newspaper. Mitch glanced up at the curtain and then back to the newspaper. He stepped away quickly and moved to where Sara was standing.

When Burton came though the curtain, he saw the couple before they saw him. He saw the young man put his hand on the girl's arm and watched as she jerked away. The hidden moments, when people don't know they're being watched, he thought, are the most revealing. It was apparent that the two were mismatched. In fact, the girl looked out of place in this town. But she was pretty in an exotic kind of way. Kind of sexy. And great legs. He looked up at her face and saw her watching him. Instantly, his demeanor switched to the polite proprietor.

"Here's my name and number. If you could ask her to think about it and call me, I would appreciate it. What was her name again?"

"Mrs. Cunningham. I'll give this to her." Mitch replied, taking the slip of paper and putting it in his pocket. "Maybe we'll bring her by tomorrow."

Burton watched as the couple walked out. This time, he remembered to lock the door.

Mitch said nothing until they got in the car.

"What was that all about?" he asked, arms folded and eyes confronting Sara.

"I don't know what you mean."

"You know exactly what I mean. This." He touched her shoulder and she flinched. "Sara, I don't know what you think I'm trying to do, but I can tell you you're wrong. Whatever or whoever you're running from has nothing to do with me. And I'm not going to try anything. In fact, I'll take you back to Jessie's right now if you want to go back."

Sara looked out the window. Why was she always saying the wrong thing, giving the wrong impression? Friendships and relationships came so easily to others. Why was she so different? She took a deep breath and turned around in the seat to face Mitch. "I didn't mean to offend you. Jessie and Frank like you a lot, so you must be a pretty decent guy. I just don't touch people, that's all."

"You don't *touch* people?" That was a new one. And it could explain the *ex*-boyfriend. Mitch thought. She certainly was unusual, but still, she intrigued him. Then he frowned, remembering why he had reached out to her earlier. "I was just trying to get your attention back there. There's something odd about that man." He paused. "I'd like to talk to Frank. When is he coming back?"

"Saturday, maybe."

"Hmm. Maybe I'll call him tonight. But don't say anything to Jessie yet. I want to think about this first."

"What are you talking about? Do you mean don't say anything about that man wanting her paintings?"

Mitch looked at her curiously, not answering. He started the car. "Let's get out of here."

Ten minutes later, Mitch turned off the highway onto a gravel road. He drove about a quarter of a mile, and pulled off the road into a shady spot. "Let's get out. I want to show you something." Before Sara could object, he walked around the car and opened her door. He started to reach for her hand to help her out, but thought better of it and put his hands in his pockets. "The creek is just on the other side of that bamboo over there. Come on, you'll see where Deer Creek gets its name."

Sara got out. It was cooler here and smelled of mud and rotting leaves. Although still muggy, the air felt cooler and cleaner than in town. She relaxed, glad for the change in both scenery and conversation. She followed him, letting him hold the branches back while she stepped carefully down a path to the water.

The creek was only about five miles from the center of the town that bore its name, but it seemed much more remote. Dense underbrush made a natural partition between the water and the road, and the water's loud rush blocked the sound of any passing car. Mitch and Sara watched the water glide over rocks, swirling and bubbling in little pools. They looked at one another and grinned.

"This is one of my favorite places," he said.

"I can see why. Do you ever see deer here?"

"Sometimes, if I come early in the morning." He watched as she walked to the edge and put her foot in the water's edge. "Careful. It's slippery." Sara bent down, took off her flip-flops, and stepped into the water. Even in the heat of June, the water was surprisingly cold.

Mitch sat down on a rock, picked up a leafy twig, and held it in the water, watching the current play with the leaves. He let it go and watched it flow downstream. His gaze turned to Sara. She was wading gingerly through the water, stopping now and then to bend over and pick up a rock. As she moved, spots on her dress glittered, mimicking the sparkling water. She stopped and stood still, closed her eyes, and breathed in the cool dampness. Standing there, she looked like a different person from the girl he'd first seen in the grocery store. It wasn't the dress, although he wasn't blind to the way it fell across her body. It was more than that. He had brought other women here. Briefly. They always complained about mosquitoes, or mud, or the heat, or the cold. Sara was different. Here, at this moment, she looked like someone who enjoyed the purity and simplicity of the creek and the rocks and the absence of all the things that made life problematic. For the first time since he'd met her, he didn't see anger in her face. No, that wasn't exactly right. When he first saw her in the grocery store, playing with the little girl, she didn't look angry or resistant. That in itself would have been normal. But it was such a contrast to her appearance that it drew his attention. Maybe he was seeing himself several years ago: rebellious and unhappy, searching. He watched her, wondering what she was thinking, who she was. For whatever reason, he wanted to know everything about her.

She opened her eyes and looked at him. "Are we in a park?"

"No, but this land is owned by the county. This area was part of the Cherokee nation years ago. Can you imagine what it must have been like then?" Mitch stood up and walked over to the water's edge, near Sara. "You asked me earlier if I liked living here. This is one of the reasons I stay. Plus Mom and friends, of course.

And the job is good. I like what I'm doing, and, for the most part, I like the people who live around here."

He wiped his hands on his shirt. "I guess we ought to go back now...And Sara, I didn't mean to discount what you were saying back in the restaurant. I guess I really don't know much about Frank's life in Knoxville. The times I've been around him, it seemed he was always focused on my family, or Jessie. He rarely talks about himself. I used to think it odd that a man his age, retired, spent so much time on his cell phone. I guess I just got used to it and stopped thinking about it." He didn't add that he knew Frank had financed some work at Jessie's house, or that everyone in town assumed Frank was the anonymous donor behind the expensive hospice addition named for his dead brother.

He started walking back to the car. Sara stepped out of the water and put on her flip-flops, suddenly remembering something he'd said earlier. "Are you going to tell me why you want to talk to Frank?"

He stopped and turned to face her, his eyes more serious than she had seen before. "Back at the gallery, I looked behind the counter when that guy went to the back room. There was a torn-out page from a newspaper with something circled. The part that was circled was a job ad. It was the same want-ad that Frank showed me."

6. THURSDAY

"Mary, it's not charity. You'll be doing a favor for someone who needs it. This lawyer friend of mine runs the program, and I told him there was an opportunity here. It won't cost you anything." Frank paused. Why did she have to be so stubborn? If he was going to sell her on the idea, he'd have to change tactics.

"Of course, if you think Bill would disapprove, I'll send my guy away. Bill should be able to come back in a week or so, maybe sooner if you push him."

"*Push him?* Frank Cunningham, you know good and well I wouldn't do anything to jeopardize Bill's health." She folded her arms and stared out the front door. Daylight was just breaking, and the sky was streaked with pink. In the early light, she could see the man Frank brought. He looked anxious.

"You say he has restaurant experience?"

"Yes. But he's been out of work for five months. He's had some bad luck." Frank saw that Mary was wavering. "He's a decent guy, and he'll work hard for you. All you have to do is keep him busy for a few months and fill out an evaluation sheet once a week."

"A FEW MONTHS? I don't need him here for months! Bill's going to get well and then he'll come back to work. The doctor said..." The woman's voice broke and she slumped into a chair. The last two days had taken a toll on her. She had never seen Bill so despondent. She didn't know much about heart attacks, but she believed a person's attitude played a large part in their recovery.

"Of course he's going to be back, and he's going to get completely well. But he's got to take it easy at first. He'll have to work up to a full day. And Mary, you're going to need a break now and then, too. You can't do this for twelve to fourteen hours a day and take care of him and yourself, too." Frank nodded his head toward the man waiting outside. "What do you say, can I tell Jackson he's got a job?"

Mary stood up and moved toward the door herself. "I imagine you already did."

***

Frank was dog-tired. Since driving back Tuesday morning, he had spent long hours at the hospital with Bill, made even longer by his friend's gloomy silence. Wednesday, he spent half a day himself at the diner making a huge mess of things before Mary arrived and got it under control. He'd gone back and spent three more hours with Bill. Last night, he'd found Jackson. Now he was sitting with his friend again, describing the diner's new cook as vaguely as possible.

"Bill, will you trust me on this? I've explained it all to Mary, and she's fine with it." He cradled his bad knee in his hands. After yesterday's activities, his knee was badly swollen and aching. What he would give to be off his feet, stretched out with a pillow under his knee and an icepack on top of it. He watched Bill punch his pillow in frustration. Frank massaged his knee and, without the slightest bit of guilt, thought how much he would appreciate a few days in bed. The thought was fleeting, though. He knew his friend was battling more than restlessness at his confinement.

Bill's reaction to his heart attack had stunned Frank. As long as he had known him, Bill had been upbeat—a glass-is-half-full type person—and this new pessimism caught Frank and Mary both by surprise. Naturally he was sympathetic. After all, it had to be a shock. One day life is a red carpet laid out before you, and the next day the carpet's been rolled up and taken away, and deep inside you know your life will never be the way it was.

Still, the dour mood and cynicism irritated Frank. For every positive comment he made, Bill had a negative reply. To top it off, now he was criticizing them for hiring Jackson.

"Could I change the subject for a while? I need your thoughts about something." Frank pulled out an envelope and handed it to his friend.

"What's this?"

"Open it and you'll see." Bill propped himself up, opened the envelope and pulled out a newspaper clipping. "That was in Sunday's *Times*," said Frank.

"So?" Bill was in no mood to discuss current events, or philosophy, or theology, or any of the usual themes of their conversations. He hated wearing the annoying blood pressure cuff. Every time he got comfortable or dosed off, the cuff would inflate and squeeze his arm. The discs stuck to his skin trailing wires from the heart monitor were annoying...and a grim reminder of the chest pains that brought him here. The IV in his arm made him feel like a prisoner. He was furious that fate had put him in a hospital bed. And he was scared for himself and for his wife. They had never had children. If he died, Mary would be all alone.

Frank pulled a chair close to the bed. "Bill," he said softly, "I know this has knocked you off your feet, but this is just a hiccup in your life." He raised his hand to stop the other man's protest. "I'm not saying it isn't serious. It is, but it's a warning, not a death sentence. A warning that you need to make some changes in your lifestyle. It's a *warning*, Bill. This," he said, sweeping his hand around the hospital room, "doesn't have to be the rest of your life. You're a young man. I know, I know, you're not a kid, anymore. But you're not old, either. And you have an incredible woman who needs you. But she doesn't need this 'you.' She needs the Bill of last week. Not a depressed and cranky man mad because life threw him a curve."

Bill's expression did not soften. If anything, he looked angrier than before. Frank sighed. "Bill Simmons, you're a lucky man. I wish I could change places with you." Bill's frown deepened. "You don't understand, and I'm not faulting you. There's no way anyone can until it starts happening. One day you try to do something—move a piece of furniture, lift a heavy box, run to get out of the rain, even climb a ladder to clean the gutters—and you find you can't do it anymore. Not only that, but you realize that you'll never, ever be able to do that thing again. It gets harder, Bill. But you're not there yet. You're not even close."

The two men stared at each other, both silent. Their posture spoke for them: Bill with his hands in fists, Frank leaning forward in his chair, one hand resting on the bed, the other arm outstretched, palms upward.

Bill spoke first. "This just isn't fair."

"*FAIR?* Of course it's not fair!" Frank's voice rose with sudden fury. "It isn't fair when disease and accidents and crimes rip through lives that should have had a chance to grow old. It's not fair for innocent children and little babies to die in earthquakes and floods and fires and tsunamis. Whatever gave you the idea that life should be fair? There is no 'fair' in this world."

He sat for several minutes, surprised at his own outburst. He sighed. He was such a hypocrite. "I'm sorry, Bill. I really do understand. I can't tell you how many times I've felt this..." he stumbled over the word... "defeated." His thoughts drifted to the agonizing days after his wife was gone. So quiet, so lonely, so empty. And then his brother. Drawing in a deep breath, he pushed away the old feelings. "It's not the end. It's never the end. Just a different life."

Calmer now, he pointed to the newspaper clipping now lying on the hospital bed. "Bill, I think this is important. I don't know why, but it worries me. Let me tell you more." He straightened up in the chair and, ignoring Bill's disinterest, explained the series of events of the past week, ending with Mitch's phone call the night before.

When he finished, Bill picked up the clipping and read it slowly, then tossed it aside. "It probably means nothing. There could be a Deer Creek in another state. The T-N might just be a typo. Maybe it was supposed to be T-X for Texas, or M-N for Minnesota."

Frank sighed, both at his friend's indifference and his own inability to understand what was going on. Maybe Bill was right. Maybe that's all it was. He picked up the empty envelope, walked to the window, and looked out. Despite his distress over Bill's heart attack and depression, he couldn't stop thinking about Deer Creek. There was something about this whole thing that bothered him. No, not *some thing*. It was all the things combined. The ad, the strange unfriendliness of the gallery man to Jessie and to him, the man's odd visit at Jessie's house, his disconcerting interest in Tony's paintings, but most importantly, Mitch's discovery of the same ad—circled—in the gallery. All the other things could be explained, but not the last.

"Or maybe..." Frank turned around at the sound of Bill's voice. The surliness was gone, if only momentarily. Bill was trying to arrange himself in a sitting position, and his face no longer had that contemptuous look. Once settled, he picked up the clipping and tapped it with his other hand. "Maybe it's some kind of message."

***

"Good morning! Today's the big day! Mr. Roberts? Are you here?" Marilyn Foster shut the door behind her and looked around for the shopkeeper. The old dress shop had converted well. She was pleased. Strange as they might be, the two men opening the gallery seemed to know what they were doing. Paintings hung on three dark taupe walls, and a cream-colored partition in the center of the room rose three-quarters of the way to the ceiling and provided more display space. The leasing agent put on her glasses and walked up to one wall, peering closely first at one painting and then at another. She didn't pretend to know much about art, but she recognized that these were tasteful and expensive.

"Hello," said a man's voice. Marilyn jumped, startled. "So, what do you think?" Burton Roberts stood three feet behind her, wearing black pants and a black and tan silk shirt, looking like she imagined a New York art dealer would look.

"This is fantastic! It's even better than I expected. I had no idea you had such an impressive inventory. Wait until people see this." Marilyn was beside herself with pride. In the last couple of weeks, she'd endured snide comments—even ridicule. Several of her friends questioned her decision in renting the store as a gallery and were speculating on how long it could stay in business. She went into commercial real estate two years ago, following a disappointing marriage and even more disappointing divorce. At 37, she was late in starting a career. She looked from one wall to another and beamed. With a bit of publicity and word of mouth, this would be a success. Maybe even transform the town. Once one shop did well, other upscale shops would want to locate nearby. Gift shops, cute little restaurants, bed and breakfasts. A shop like this could bring in tourists from the nearby cities. She, of course, would be given the credit for starting it. This little shop could be the turning point for her own future.

"I have to call our newspaper editor. I'm sure he will want to run a story on you for our little paper—take pictures, too."

"Photos?" The proprietor looked uneasy. "Oh, I don't know if that would be such a good idea."

"Well why not?" asked Marilyn. "I'm sure you're accustomed

to dealing with big city art critics, but you'll find our newspaper is good, for a town this size. And our new editor is good, too. When he took over, he stopped running those ridiculous small-town silly articles, like whose grandchildren were in town for a visit, and started running real news. Why, he will probably want to carry a story about your shop on the business page. It would be free advertising for you."

"Yes, of course, a story would be good," he conceded, "but no photographs. You see, photos would require permission from the artists. Copyright infringement—that sort of thing. The paperwork would simply be a nightmare." He threw up his hands in mock exasperation.

She nodded vigorously and said she would see to it that the newsman came over, sans camera, to cover the opening. After looking at every painting and gushing non-stop, she told him she was going right then to find the newspaper editor.

As she turned to leave, the man stopped her. "Ms. Foster, do you by chance know an older woman named Mrs. Cunningham?"

"Why of course, I've known Jessie for years. Why?"

"Just curious. She came in one day and accidentally left a bag here. When I took it to her, I saw that she had some very unusual paintings in her home."

Marilyn's eyes narrowed. "Oh, yes. Her husband had peculiar taste. People were just shocked when she hung up those pictures for everyone to see. Some, as you must have seen, are quite, uh, shall we say, sensual? And she lets her *grandchildren* see them!" Marilyn stopped suddenly, aware of the amusement on his face. She tried to backtrack, not wanting him to think she wasn't sophisticated. "Of course, art is different things to different people. I just don't want poor Jessie to be talked about behind her back."

"And you, Marilyn, do you like, as you say, 'sensual' art?" he asked, moving closer to her as he now called her by her first name. Marilyn felt her face redden. She didn't know if he was making fun of her, or if he was flirting. Flirting? Maybe she had misinterpreted him and his partner. Maybe they were just business partners after all.

Confused, flustered—and flattered—Marilyn feigned innocence and changed the subject. "Did you want to ask me something about Jessie?"

Burton smiled, pleased at her discomfort. "Yes. I was wondering if any of the art was original."

"Oh, yes. It's all original," she said matter-of-factly.

"*It is?* She told me that her husband collected art, but she seems like such an, uh, ordinary person." He hesitated, then as tactfully as he could, asked, "Was her husband well-off?"

"Hmm. Don't know for sure. But after he died, the hospice here added on a big extension and named something after him. There was a story in the paper about it. The addition cost a bundle. But all anyone would say was that it was paid for by an anonymous donor. Most people just assumed it was from family money, though. Lord knows, to talk to Jessie, you'd think the only thing of value to her are those paintings." She looked at him with curiosity. "Why are you interested?"

He repeated the story he'd told yesterday. "I want to ask her if she'd agree to let me display some of the work here, a temporary exhibit. It's an unusual collection, and I thought it might bring in traffic to the gallery."

Marilyn mulled this over and nodded her head seriously. "That's a smart move. I'm sure Jessie would agree. She loves to show off the paintings and talk about them. But I'd be careful if I were you. Some people around town aren't as progressive as you and I are. You wouldn't want to offend anyone."

With that, she said she was going to the editor's office and left the shop. As she walked out, she felt him watching her, and put a little sway in her hips. As he watched her sashay out the door, Jake Burton, a.k.a. Burton Roberts, sat down on the stool behind the counter and, for the first time in weeks, wondered just what in the hell he was doing.

***

"I don't know if I believe in a heaven." *However did this happen,* Sara wondered. A polite question about Jessie's day at the hospice had morphed into this serious conversation. "I mean, just think of how many people there have been since the beginning of time. How could there be that much room? And what about the animals?" she asked, reaching down to scratch Gracie under her chin. "If there was a heaven, it would have to include the animals, and how could there be room for all the animals that have ever lived?"

Jessie chuckled and Sara frowned. "You're laughing at me."

"No, no, no. I was just imagining Gracie here meeting up with a T. Rex."

"Okay, forget the animals for a minute. Think of the huge numbers of people that are and have been and ever will be."

Jessie mulled that over for a moment. "Yes, that would be something, wouldn't it? Sort of like the Internet."

"*What?*"

"The Internet. It's endless, no limits."

Sara laughed, and, satisfied, the two retuned to watering the flowers and grapevines.

***

Frank hauled himself out of the car and tiredly walked up to Jessie's front door. He felt encouraged about Bill. They had talked more and he left his friend in better spirits. Although not completely his old self, Bill seemed to be trying, and that was the first step. The new cook was going to work out just fine for Mary. Before he left, he'd tied up loose ends on several business projects. Now maybe he could focus on matters here.

He rang the bell. No one answered. He tried the door. Locked. Hearing laughter coming from the back yard, he left the porch and made his way around the house. There he saw Jessie and Sara, their backs to him. He watched as Jessie pointed out flowers and Sara nimbly bent over to touch or smell them. Sometimes he could remember being that young and agile. When the girl turned her face to Jessie, Frank thought she looked somewhat different, less harsh. The blue streaks in her hair looked less garish than before. It made him think of the bruises that sometimes appeared out of nowhere on his aging body, then faded away. He seldom could recall what caused them… he was always bumping into something. At first he found the bruises hideous, insulting actually, making him feel like a piece of fruit beginning to rot. Now he just enjoyed the show, tracking the changing colors and new patterns and watching them fade away, just like time. If only people knew what was in store for them, how differently would they live, he wondered. Just look at Jessie and Sara. Years ago, Jessie was a girl that age. Years to come, Sara would be Jessie's age. He smiled at the image of an old Sara with blue bangs.

Just then, Sara saw him and waved. Jessie turned and Frank thought she looked especially glad to see him. The women walked over to him and Jessie hugged him tightly. He hugged her back, and was almost embarrassed by the emotion he felt. Sometimes he wished he could turn off the thoughts that were forever racing around his head. They made him overly sentimental. Or perhaps he was just more tired than he realized.

"I didn't hear you drive up," Jessie said. She pulled away and her smile disappeared when she saw his drawn face. "Francis, you look exhausted. Let's go inside, out of this heat. Here, let Sara take your bag," she said, relieving Frank of the small duffle bag he was carrying and handing it to the girl. Frank was uncomfortable with the attention the women were giving him, but he *was* tired. So he let them lead him inside and settle him into a kitchen chair. Two minutes later, the ubiquitous iced tea was on the table, then potato salad and sandwiches.

Frank caught them up on Bill's state, and just as he finished, there was a knock at the back door. Before Jessie could rise, Sara jumped up and opened the door. It was Mitch.

"I was driving by and saw Frank's car," Mitch said. "You didn't hear me at the front, so I came around back." From the doorway,

Mitch could easily see Frank and Jessie. But his eyes remained on Sara.

"Mitch, I was about to suggest that we call you," Frank said. "Sit down. We need to talk. We need to fill in Jessie on what's happened."

"Happened? What's happened?" asked Jessie.

Mitch told Jessie of his and Sara's visit to the gallery yesterday, and seeing the newspaper clipping. Jessie looked at Sara in surprise. "I asked her not to tell you," Mitch interceded. "I didn't want to worry you, and I wanted to do a little research first." He glanced at Frank. "But I did call Frank last night, and he agreed that we should tell you everything we know."

"Unfortunately, that's all we know," added Frank. "Except for Bill's idea."

"Bill?" the other three all said simultaneously.

"I wanted someone else's opinion," he answered simply. "He suggested the ad might contain a hidden message."

He got up and got the envelope with the clipping from his bag and sat back down. They passed it around, throwing out ideas of how a message could be hidden in the ad.

"You said you did some research," Sara said to Mitch. "What kind of research?"

"I googled the man at the gallery, and I tried to find him in our database—but I didn't tell the sheriff, so please let's keep this to ourselves. I couldn't find anyone named Burton Roberts."

"If that's his real name," Frank said.

Jessie felt a chill go through her. "Lord have mercy," she said.

They all looked at one another, the feeling growing between them that something mysterious and malevolent lurked nearby.

Mitch spoke next. "Let's say it is a coded message. Why? Drugs? That's a lot of trouble for a drug deal. Guys sell drugs every day, everywhere. It's easy to find buyers and sellers. And why use a newspaper ad when everyone has cell phones and email? Also, if this ad were about drugs, it would have to be about a huge transaction. I just don't think that's what it is." He paused. "And if I took this to the sheriff with just the ad to go on, I'd be the laughingstock of the office. So, if not drugs, then what? What else would be worth an elaborate scheme of placing this ad—and two total strangers coming here to open an art gallery of all things? None of it makes sense."

Prior to their phone conversation the previous night, Frank had not considered any link between the ad and the gallery. Now he couldn't separate them. He spoke solemnly. "I think we should all go to the gallery this afternoon and look around, talk to the man, or men, again, and see if we can pick up on anything."

"You mean look for clues?" Jessie asked.

"Yes," Frank answered. "I brought three of Bill's wooden boxes back with me. That can be an excuse to have another conversation with this Mr. Roberts. I'll ask him if he wants to buy them, and try to work in some more questions."

"And Sara and I can go separately," Mitch added. "I need to run home and change. I don't want to go there in uniform." He looked at Sara. "Why don't you come with me now and we'll go straight there from my place—to save time. Then the four of us can regroup tonight and compare notes. I'll bring a couple of pizzas."

"Pizza?" Frank frowned. Even through all the turmoil of the day, he had been secretly hoping for a home-cooked meal.

Jessie stifled a laugh. These two were so transparent. It was plain as day that Mitch wanted to be alone with Sara, and it was equally plain that pizza was not what Francis wanted for supper. She thought quickly, then spoke. "Actually, I was going to fix beef stew and cornbread tonight. Of course, you're all welcome to join me, but since Sara doesn't eat meat, why don't you kids come back here after your pizza and we'll rehash everything over pie and coffee? And Francis, I think it'd be a good idea if you iced your knee for a while and rested before we go over there." Jessie looked past them, out the window and toward the gallery. As quickly as it came, her good mood vanished. What, she thought, was happening in her quiet, peaceful town?

***

Frank woke with a start. It took him several seconds to remember where he was, even what day it was. He sat up and swung his legs off the couch where he had fallen asleep. As soon as his feet touched the floor, Gracie jumped up where his feet had been, sniffed several times, turned in a circle, and sat down, glaring at him and emitting a low growl.

"Oh, give it a rest," he said with irritation.

Just then, Jessie walked into the room. "I'm sorry, Francis. I don't know why she's that way around you." She sat down. "I'm glad you fell asleep. You needed it."

Frank looked at his watch. He had slept less than an hour, but he felt refreshed. He remembered the gallery and their earlier conversation. "I guess we should get going. They may be closing soon," he said.

"Yes. I've been thinking about it, and I really don't know what I should say."

"We can both carry the boxes, let him look at them, and ask if he'll take them on consignment. Maybe ask the men where they're from, just small talk. I don't have any real plan. Let's just go and see what happens."

She looked grim. "Just don't leave me alone with either of them. I don't like confrontations. Yellow is my favorite color."

***

Fewer than a dozen visitors had come into the shop on the opening day. Burton was relieved. He was waiting for a phone call and hoped the shop would be empty when it came.

The curvy real estate woman had been back and, true at her word, brought the newspaper guy with her. He got rid of them after about 20 minutes and felt no damage had been done. Neither of them seemed to have much knowledge of art. The man took a few notes, asked how many customers had been in, and asked him to describe the types of artwork on display.

He thought of Marilyn Foster again. She wasn't extraordinarily pretty, but she was an attractive and shapely woman. He recalled her first description of the Cunningham woman's paintings. *Sensual*, she had said. Although she'd meant it as a criticism, she was correct. Marc Chagall was Burton's favorite artist. He liked the brilliant colors, the floating lovers, and comical violin-playing horses and fish. He had never understood why Chagall's works weren't as astronomically expensive as those of some other artists. Picasso, for example. His Cubism work was hard and sterile. Chagall took Cubism, softened the edges, and made it come alive with whimsical, erotic images.

He thought of the two boxes he had stashed away and smiled.

The door chimed and he looked up. It was the Cunningham woman. "Good afternoon," he said eagerly, thinking that opportunity was again his for the taking.

"Hello," the woman said quietly. To his disappointment, an older man followed her in.

"Mr. Roberts, good to see you again," said her companion. "Remember me? We spoke about the band saw boxes. I brought three for you to see." Without waiting for a response, Frank walked to the empty counter and pulled three wrapped items from a paper sack. "I'm sure you'll agree that they are beautiful works." As he began to unwrap one package, he looked around, nodding his head appreciatively. "This is quite nice. You've done a wonderful job. Had many people in today?"

Burton looked from the man to woman, who had turned her attention to the paintings. He wished she had come in alone, but maybe he could turn this to his advantage.

"Yes, it's been quite an interesting day," he said. "Let's see what you have."

One by one, Frank carefully unwrapped and set the boxes on the counter, then pulled from his shirt pocket small cards with Bill's name and a brief description of the persimmon wood art. He placed a card inside each box.

This time, Burton didn't have to fake his interest. The quality was excellent, and the carvings were not only unique but quite delicate considering the hard wood. The material itself was interesting, dark and dense.

"I was hoping you'd be willing to display these for a couple of weeks, on a consignment basis of course. Is that how you did it in your last shop?" When the man didn't answer, Frank continued, "Perhaps you could suggest a price and a consignment percentage?"

Burton vaguely remembered ringing up sales of similar works items in the L.A. or New Orleans galleries but he couldn't immediately recall their prices. Painting was his preferred art form. They were more lucrative, more coveted by most collectors. "Let me discuss it with my partner and get back to you," he said, adding, "They are extraordinary pieces. I'm sure we can work out something agreeable to all of us." He held out his hand to Frank and the men shook on the nebulous deal.

When he felt that he had said enough about the boxes, Burton spoke to the woman. "Mrs. Cunningham, how do you like our selections?"

Jessie turned at the sound of her name, gathered up her courage, and looked at the man. "They're beautiful. It's quite a collection."

Indeed, thought Burton. Aloud, he said, "I don't know if word got to you, but I did mention to a neighbor of yours that I would love to display a few pieces from your own collection. As an on-loan exhibit." The stunned look on her face told him she had not gotten the message. "It would only be for a short period of time, to share it with the community." She was frowning. "It would be a public service, very educational. Later, I hope to show works by local artists, perhaps art students from schools. Starting with your display and your friend's wooden boxes, I believe the gallery could quickly contribute to the community—show people that art is for everyone."

"No," Jessie said firmly. "They're much too valuable."

Burton almost gasped. Controlling his voice, he said, "Don't make a decision right now. Please consider it for a few days."

Frank listened, confused. What was going on here? Things weren't going according to his plan. They weren't learning anything about this man, Jessie was getting agitated and uncomfortable, and he'd better do something to regain control of the conversation.

"Jessie, that's a good suggestion. There's no need to decide on the spot. Think about it for a couple of days. It might be fun to have your own display here." Jessie looked at him with astonishment, but was too annoyed to reply. Frank noisily wadded up the sack and wrapping paper and, moving toward the back room, asked if there was a trashcan in the back.

Burton quickly took the paper from him and put it under the counter. "I'll take care of it later."

Frank left the counter and steered Jessie toward one of the partitions, pointing out an elaborately framed landscape. He looked back at Burton and smiled innocently. "Tell me, Mr. Roberts, are you from this part of the country?"

***

Karen headed toward the living room when she heard the front door open. "Mitch?"

"Yeah, Mom, it's me."

Karen rounded the corner and stopped. Standing next to her handsome son was a young woman. Karen took in the blue hair, piercings, heavy eyeliner, and bright blue nail polish. This had to be Sara. Jessie's description was right on the money.

"This is my mom," Mitch said, "and Mom, this is Sara. I'm going to change, and then we're going back to town for a little while. I promised her pizza tonight, so don't plan on me for supper."

"Nice to meet you, Sara. I was just working in the kitchen. Come on back and sit with me while Mitch gets ready."

Mitch rolled his eyes. "Sara, don't eat anything that doesn't come pre-cooked and in a wrapper."

"Don't pay any attention to him," Karen said. She walked into the kitchen and Sara followed. Karen went to the stove and stirred something in a saucepan. Smoke drifted up from it, along with smells of curry and coconut. Sara leaned against the counter opposite from her, observing the woman. Karen was younger than Sara expected her to be, much younger than Jessie. She was trim, stylish, and had golden-brown hair that swung a couple of inches above her shoulders. She had the same dark brown eyes as Mitch—and she was simply beautiful. Although she was ashamed to think it, she couldn't help but wonder what this gorgeous woman and plain Jessie had in common to make them such good friends. She was suddenly aware of her chipped nail polish and slipped her hands in her jeans pockets.

"I hear that you've been helping out Jessie this week."

"Yes."

"I know she really appreciates it. She says you've been a great help. You know, I'm glad you've been there these past few days. Jessie needed the company."

"I've enjoyed it."

"I wish her children could visit her more. I worry about her being alone so much." She stirred the pan, patiently waiting for Sara to speak. After a couple minutes of awkward silence, Karen tried again. "Jessie said you're from Savannah?"

"Yes."

"I've never been there, but I've read lots about it. It sounds like a great place to live."

"Yes."

"Are you in school, or have you already graduated?"

"Last year of college."

"How long are you staying in Deer Creek?"

"Mom, stop giving her the third degree." Mitch walked into the kitchen and to the stove, looked into the pan and winced. "Want me to bring back enough pizza for you?"

"No thanks. I'm having this." She tasted the mixture and put down her spoon. "Well, maybe a small pepperoni... just in case."

Mitch grinned and told her they'd be back in a couple of hours. After they left, Karen watched them out the window, staring until they drove away. They didn't hold hands or act like they were on a date, but Karen had glimpsed something in Mitch that she hadn't seen before. It wasn't much, just the way he looked at the girl. Or, more accurately, the way he didn't look at her. Mitch had dated every unmarried girl in town at least once. Most were as pretty if not prettier than Sara. And with each one, he always found something to complain about. Something told her that this time was different.

Actually, she realized, Mitch hadn't told her about Sara. Thank God Jessie had prepared her. The girl seemed nice enough, and Jessie liked her and that carried a lot of weight. Still, Karen couldn't help but recall Mitch's wild high school days and some of the troubled kids who she felt were bad influences on him. But that was years ago. Mitch was all grown up now, a man making a man's decisions. Suddenly she didn't know whether to laugh or cry. She just hoped Sara was as special as her son seemed to think she was.

***

"Here's what I thought we'd do: go to the gallery, walk around and pretend to be interested in buying something, make some small talk, ask how Deer Creek compares to other places they've lived and worked—you know, work in a few questions to try to find out something about these men. Then we'll get a pizza, maybe drop off something for Mom, and go back to Jessie's."

Sara knew he was talking to her, but she only heard part of what he was saying. Her mind was still back in his mother's kitchen, replaying the easy banter between the woman and her son.

"Hello in there. Are you listening?"

She shook her head. "No… I mean, yes." She sighed. "You'd better tell me again."

Mitch looked into her eyes and said solemnly, "Just go along with me."

Sara nodded mutely, and in one dazzling moment, realized that was just what she wanted.

***

First the old couple, now the odd couple again, Burton chuckled to himself. He watched the pair as they wandered about, pretending to be interested in each painting. How many times had he observed men and women as they tried to impress each other with their knowledge of art when it was obvious they didn't know a Turner from a Degas? At least these two asked questions; they didn't insult his intelligence by trying to tell him what they knew.

The girl was less talkative. Too bad, he'd like to talk to her. He watched her as she looked closely at one of the landscapes. As she leaned toward it, she raised both arms and tucked her hair behind her ears, causing her shirt to hike up and show a taut, bare waist above tight jeans. He caught himself staring and quickly turned away. Just at that moment, the cell phone clipped to his belt rang. "Excuse me," he said, and walked to the back of the room. He spoke quietly into the phone and slipped behind the curtain.

Several minutes later, he emerged from the back. The couple was still there, now leaning against the counter and fingering the wooden boxes. He put on his shopkeeper's smile. "Those just came in today and we're still negotiating prices. If you're interested, I can give you a call tomorrow."

"Oh, that's okay. We'll come back in a couple of days," Mitch said.

After they left, Burton waited a minute, then locked the door, turned out the light, and walked to the back.

***

"He gives me the creeps," Jessie said.

"There is something odd about the place," Mitch added, "or maybe just him. "But I can't put my finger on it. What did you think, Sara?"

Sara sat up straighter, pleased that he asked her opinion. She hesitated, wanting to be helpful but afraid they—mostly Mitch—might misinterpret her comments. "I agree with Jessie. He gives me the creeps, too." There was also something disingenuous about him. She recalled the gay classmates she had known in high school and college and their efforts to fit in, not stand out. "What's really weird is that he's giving people the impression that he and his business partner are a gay couple. We never saw the other man, but this man isn't gay, at least I don't think he is. Why would a man want people to think that he is? The artwork is beautiful, it looks really classy and expensive, but the man seems a little sketchy." Sara stopped talking. The others were looking at her intently. She wondered if she sounded foolish.

Mitch spoke first. "You know, I thought the same thing… both times we were in the gallery." He glanced across the kitchen table at Frank and Jessie and explained, "It was the way he looked at Sara—too appreciatively."

Although she flushed, Sara was pleased that he had noticed.

"Francis, you've been awfully quiet," said Jessie. "You've hardly said anything all evening."

Frank looked up in surprise. "Oh, Jessie, I'm so sorry." He put his hand over Jessie's, and looked at her with concern. "Have I been rude? Supper was delicious, and this lemon pie is incredible. I let you do all that work and didn't even thank you for it. I was so preoccupied with this situation."

She looked at him tenderly. He was such a good man. She was so glad to have him in her life, and these two youngsters, too. How could anything really wrong or bad happen around her when she was surrounded by people like these? Mitch was talking now, and she and Frank turned to him.

"Did you learn anything while you were there?" Mitch asked them.

"No, he didn't answer any of my questions, not really. He sounded knowledgeable about the art, but he didn't give any clue as to where he was from or what he did before he came here. To tell you the truth, he just seemed interested in Jessie's paintings."

Mitch frowned. "We didn't learn anything either," he said. "Just before we left, he got a call on his cell and went in the back to talk. When he came back, he looked a little excited, like he had gotten some good news. We left, and after we walked out, I heard him lock the door and we saw him turn out the lights. It could have been a coincidence. The phone call could have been anyone, and maybe he was just ready to close up for the day."

Frank nodded in agreement. "We just don't know enough. So let's go over what we do know; maybe something will click. First, there's the want ad in the paper. That's definitely odd. I've been thinking about that a lot and I believe Bill may be right, that it is some sort of coded message. But, like you said before, why put it in a newspaper? Why not use the Internet and email? Or just make a phone call? I hate to say it, but most people don't buy newspapers anymore.

"Second, suppose you're right, Sara, and these men deliberately let people think they are a couple. Why? Would it be so that most folks here in a small town would leave them alone? And if that's the case, why? They can't build customers that way… unless they aren't here for that reason."

Mitch thought of the known drug users in the county. He hadn't noticed any unusual activity recently. "I've gone over the arrest sheets and complaints for the past three weeks, looking for some change in drug activity." Turning to Sara, he said, "Even in a little town like ours, drugs are a problem. But nothing seems to be going on. I just don't think it's drugs. And if it's not drugs, then what? Guns, prostitution, some kind of fraud? I just can't figure out what to look for. And I still haven't said anything to the sheriff."

"I think you're right," Frank said. "We have to figure this out. Let's go back to the ad."

A light knock on the back door startled them all. Sara was closest, so she got up, turned on the porch light and, opening the door, said, "Mitch, it's your mom."

As they made room around the table for Karen, Frank slipped the newspaper ad back into his jacket. Jessie cut her a slice of pie. Mitch and Sara sat silently.

"What's going on?" Karen asked. "You all look like you got caught doing something illegal." When no one answered, Karen said, "I was just making a joke."

They looked at each other. Jessie spoke up. "I think we should tell Karen what's happened. Maybe she'll have an idea—like Bill did. Besides, Karen has read more mystery novels than all of us put together. And she already knows about that man coming over here."

"You're right," said Frank. "Karen, read this." He pulled the ad from his pocket and handed it to her. She read it, and looked up, more puzzled than before. They spent the next five minutes telling her all that they had seen and heard, and another ten minutes describing their vague suspicions about the gallery and its owners.

"Mitch, can you check their backgrounds?"

"You're assuming they have a criminal history," Mitch replied. "And yes, I tried, and nothing came up under their names. Actually, I don't have anything else to look up." Mitch stopped cold, grimaced, and shook his head. "I can't believe I didn't think of this before. I can run their license plate. I've only seen one car, and it was parked in the back. Jessie, do you know if you can see their tag from your window?"

"I don't know. The shrubbery might block it. I'll look in the morning and call you."

"Does anyone have any other ideas?" Frank asked.

"What about Marilyn Foster?" Karen said. "She's the one who has dealt with them the most, renting the property to them. It seems as though she would have done a credit check on them, or something."

"Good idea, Mom. Do you think you could pump her for information without letting her know that's what you're doing?"

Karen laughed. "Of course I can, Mitch. How else could I have kept tabs on you all these years?"

"Okay," he said, ignoring her attempt at humor. Sometimes he wondered if she realized he wasn't still in high school. "Give it a try, and let me know if you learn anything. Can you talk to her in the morning?"

"I'll look her up around lunchtime after I leave hospice. Jessie, that's one reason I dropped by—can you work three hours tomorrow? Annie is still too sick to come in."

"Well, yes, I guess so. Francis, Sara, do you mind being on your own for breakfast?"

"Not a problem," said Sara. "I'll handle it."

Frank was pleased. Amid all this turmoil, this strangeness that had fallen upon them, it seemed to him that Sara was coming together—"finding herself" is what the kids used to call it. The anger within her seemed to be slipping away. He couldn't have been prouder of her if she were his own daughter—or granddaughter for that matter. He looked around the table. Everyone was quiet now, thoughtful. He looked at this unusual group and thought how fate had put them together. A different decision somewhere in the past could have kept them apart, changed their lives forever. He must be tired, he thought. He didn't usually get so philosophical. The day was taking its toll on him and he yawned, unable to hide his weariness.

Jessie had been watching him and, weary herself, suggested they call it a night and regroup the next day. "Let's meet at my house," Karen said. "I'll fix dinner for all of us." The others agreed, and Mitch made a mental note to stop for a burger before dinner.

The older women made quick plans for the next morning. Frank excused himself to make a phone call to check on Bill, said goodnight to all, and took his overnight bag to the bedroom.

Restless, Sara cleared the table of the dessert plates and began washing them in the sink. Without saying a word, Mitch picked up a dishcloth and joined her. Neither noticed when Jessie and Karen left the kitchen.

After the last dish was dried and put away, Mitch leaned back against the counter. He looked to be sure they were alone, then asked, "Do you get bored here? I mean, Jessie and Frank are wonderful, but it must be kind of strange for you, without your friends and family around."

Sara wondered if her friends had even noticed she was gone. Not that she could blame them. It had been weeks—or was it months?—since she paid them any attention. She couldn't pinpoint when it started, sometime after she started seeing Alex. He made fun of her friends, said they were snobbish and thought they were better than him. She defended them at first, but after a while, she found it easier to avoid her friends.

Alex also told her she was a daddy's girl and needed to break away and be her own person. Her dad told her that Alex was a phony and a loser, which made her all the more defiant. Looking back, she felt a great sense of loss. She missed her friends. She missed her dad. Even thinking about his girlfriend didn't bother her. Her dad had been alone for years, well, not counting being in the house with her of course. Why shouldn't he find someone to share his life?

"Earth to Sara."

"Sorry, I was thinking."

"Yeah, well, I didn't mean to make you homesick. I guess you'd rather be back in Savannah than here." The way he said it was more of a question than a statement, and the intensity in his eyes made her look away.

Nervously, she looked down and absent-mindedly began picking at the last bit of nail polish left on her thumb.

"Hey, I just remembered," Mitch said, grinning. "I bought you something today." She looked at him curiously as he reached in his pants pocket and pulled out first his keys, then a small bottle of nail polish. He handed it to her, watching for a reaction.

Sara took the bottle and held it up to the light, watching speckles of silver glitter run through a deep navy polish. A smile stretched across her face.

"It's called Midnight Sky."

"I love it!" Sara said excitedly. "I can't believe you bought this for me."

"I noticed that all the work you've been doing for Jessie messed up your nails. That must sound weird coming from a guy...guess that comes from living with Mom. She's always fussing with her nails or changing hairstyles. Anyway, I was thinking that Jessie probably didn't keep stuff like this around the house and that maybe you'd like it."

"Thank you, Mitch. That was really sweet."

He smiled back at her. "I thought you'd like the color. You seem to like blue." He paused, then motioned to the table. "Let's sit...unless you think I should go."

Sara shook her head, sat down at the table and motioned for him to sit across from her. She shook the polish, but before she could twist off the cap, he took it from her.

"Let me."

"What?"

"Let me," he repeated. Sara stared at him for a few seconds, then a look of astonishment came over her face as she realized what he meant. "Oh, come on," he said, "I've painted more model cars and airplanes than you have fingernails. And just think of how impressed your girlfriends will be when you tell them you had the tough sheriff's deputy doing this girly stuff for you."

With that, he picked up her right hand. This time, she didn't pull away.

7. FRIDAY

Frank woke around six-thirty, dressed hurriedly, and went to the living room. Looking outside, he saw that Jessie's car was still in the driveway. He found her in the kitchen, a mostly eaten slice of lemon pie in front of her. Dessert for breakfast? He liked the idea.

"Why, good morning, Francis. Did I wake you? I was trying to be quiet so you could sleep in while I'm at hospice."

He shook his head and held up a pen and piece of paper. "No, I just woke up. Actually, I woke up thinking about the license plate number. I thought I'd go out early so you wouldn't have to do it."

Jessie's smile faded and she put down her fork, her appetite gone. "I had forgotten. I'll walk out with you."

As they walked toward the back of the yard, Frank whispered, "Pretend to be looking for grapes, just in case he sees us. And if we see the plate, you remember the first four numbers and I'll remember the rest. Then we'll write it down when we go back in."

"Aren't you being just a little melodramatic?" Jessie asked. "No one would believe we're out here picking grapes when the sun is just barely up." Nevertheless, she avoided looking toward the second story of the building across the alley. When they got to the muscadine vines, Jessie picked a few grapes, wet with dew, while glancing through the slits in the fence. By holding back some vines with his cane, Frank could see over Jessie's fence and into the alley. There was no fence around the other property to obstruct their view. There was also no car.

As they turned and walked back to the house, across the alley and twenty feet up, a faded yellow curtain silently closed.

***

There must have been a dozen vases, all in various sizes and shapes, lined up on the bedside table, the window sill, even on the floor. Zinnias shone their brilliant oranges and reds. Petunias spilled over the vase tops in drapes of purple. Yellow marigolds offered their distinct fragrance from one side of the room, and a clumsy bouquet of honeysuckle competed with its perfume from the other side. Gerald must have run out of vases, Jessie thought, for two soda cans held a handful of daisies and red begonias. She smiled at the sight, until she saw the tears rolling down the old man's face. Quietly, she backed out of the room into the hallway, softly closing the door to give them their privacy. She walked to the nurse's station to alert Alice.

"Don't cry," the old woman said weakly. "I'm ready...I wish..." She stopped, closing her eyes.

"What, dear? You want water? A pill for pain? I'll get the nurse." He rose to go, but his wife squeezed his hand and he stopped.

Her eyes opened and searched his face. She loved that face. It was the deeply lined face of a man who had worked outdoors his entire life, had risen before daylight each day, kissed his wife good-bye, and came home ten hours later, either sweaty from the heat or numb from the cold. His life was little different from millions of others, but like so many good, decent lives, it got little notice from a world obsessed with glitz and glamour.

"No, I want nothing," she said. "All these days here, watching you come in every morning... the flowers... I've thought about our lives." She was having trouble getting the words out. She was afraid her time would end before she could say it. With great effort, she spoke. "You... always had to work so hard... I did so little... couldn't do much to help pay for things... I wish I had been a better wife."

The man looked at her with tenderness. "Oh Hazel, don't say that. You've been a wonderful wife. No man could ask for more. You took care of the children, the house, you took care of us. I made the living, but you—*you*—made the living worthwhile. I... I don't know what I'll do without you. I love you so."

The woman's face relaxed and, with great effort, she whispered, "Love... you."

***

Frank was on his third cup of coffee and fourth phone call when Sara came into the kitchen. "Sounds great," he said into his cell phone. "I'll call you back tomorrow with details...Yes. I'm sure. Good, good. You won't be sorry." He put down the phone and wrote something in a small spiral notebook. He was about to make another call when he realized Sara was standing in the doorway.

"Hey," she said, giving him an unexpected smile.

He looked at her quizzically. She was wearing what had to be one of Jessie's old cotton bathrobes, drawn around her and tied with a mismatched belt. But it wasn't the old robe that made her look different. It was the first time he'd seen her when her eyes weren't outlined in black. Even sleepy-eyed, she looked pretty. "Good morning," he said. Sara sat down across from him and yawned. She tried to suppress it, the result a peculiar noise that made her laugh at herself. Frank put his phone down and looked at her, his bushy eyebrows raised in a question.

"What?" she said.

"You woke up awfully happy."

"Yeah, I guess so." She spread her fingers out in front of her, and he noticed that her nails were now a shiny dark blue. She looked at them and smiled and, with another yawn coming on, this time she covered her mouth. She motioned to his notebook and phone. "What are you up to today? Something about the gallery?"

"Oh no, just a little work I do from time to time. But speaking of the gallery, Jessie and I went outside this morning. Their car was gone, so there was no license number to give to Mitch. If you hear from him today, tell him we'll try again later." Her face reddened and he watched as she got up and walked to the refrigerator, still smiling to herself. Frank didn't have to ask. He had seen that look so many times among the students in his classes. He thought about the glances between Sara and Mitch last night and remembered hearing Mitch leave very late. The changes he'd been seeing in Sara since returning to Jessie's weren't at all about maturity, he realized with disappointment. What he believed last night to be a transformation in attitude, a shedding of emotional baggage, was simply a schoolgirl crush. She'd just moved her attention from one man to another. That was no solution. Granted, Mitch was a good kid, well, not a kid any more, old enough to know better. Somebody was going to get hurt here and Frank didn't think it would be the young deputy. He suddenly regretted bringing Sara to Deer Creek.

"You haven't had breakfast yet, have you?" she asked, looking dreamily into the refrigerator.

"Yes, but that was several hours ago. I could eat again. We could have cereal, or I could go pick up something, maybe donuts or sausage-biscuits. Or, for you, biscuits with no sausage."

"Oh, that's too much bother for you. Just go ahead with your work. I'll fix us something." Sara took out the milk and eggs and went to the cabinet, humming to herself.

Frank sat for a moment longer, then gathered his notebook, pen, and cell phone and went into the next room, where he spread his things on the coffee table and settled himself into a chair.

He wasn't sure he'd be able to concentrate on his calls in this room either, surrounded by his brother's artwork. The pictures weren't what he would call soothing. In fact, when he looked at them, he could envision the amusement in his brother's eyes and hear his infectious laughter. True, Frank had encouraged Jessie to hang the paintings, and he paid experts to ensure they were displayed handsomely. But he did it for Jessie and Tony, not for any love of art. Their mother loved paintings and had encouraged both sons to appreciate the arts; it was a gene that skipped him and fell on Tony. Still, he enjoyed being in the room, even if it was distracting; he felt close to Tony there.

Just as he picked up his phone, he heard Sara's off-key voice from the kitchen, singing. "*New places, new faces...I turned around and you were there...Starting over, fields of clover...I stumbled, you caught me, I fell...Me and you, now there's two...Who knew what starting over could bring...*"

Frank groaned. He needed to have a talk with Mitch, and quickly. But first things first. Once again, he gathered up his work and headed toward the bedroom, hoping Sara's discordant singing wouldn't follow him into that part of the house. Apparently Gracie felt the same, for as Frank entered the bedroom, Gracie ran before him and crawled under his bed.

***

After the funeral home personnel left, and Mr. Yarbrough with them, Jessie checked on each remaining patient. Most were aware of the early morning's events, and she wanted to make sure that other patients or family members were not upset. Even in this environment, she knew that people handled death differently. For the uninitiated, their first encounter was often shock or outrage at fate's seeming indifference. Those who had faced it before recognized that life's march can be halted at any time, regardless of goodness, age, or contributions made or left to be made.

Jessie found Albert Perry outside, sitting alone and reading. His breathing was labored, but his demeanor was peaceful. He greeted her with a nod and patted the bench beside him. As she sat down, he asked, "Have you ever read Oscar Wilde?"

"No, not that I remember. Why?"

"Listen to this quote from him: '*Death must be so beautiful. To lie in the soft brown earth, with the grasses waving above one's head, and listen to silence. To have no yesterday, and no tomorrow. To forget time, to forgive life, to be at peace.*' That sounds so nice, so calm."

"Yes, it does sound calm, but maybe a bit boring, don't you think? I like Van Gogh's thoughts on death." Albert shook his head vaguely, so she continued, "He speculated that just as living people use trains or whatever to travel about on earth, that perhaps in death we use disease or illness or old age to travel to the stars." Her eyes twinkled. "It makes one look at his Starry Night painting in a whole different light, doesn't it?"

The corners of his mouth lifted ever so slightly. "What do you think, Jessie? Do you believe we'll have a life after death?"

"Why, of course I do, Albert, don't you?"

"I guess so. I hope so. When you've been told your whole life that there is a heaven and a hell, it seems unnatural, or wrong, not to believe it." He paused, closing his book. "Still, I've never accepted the idea of one religious group having a better shot at getting to heaven than all the other groups. That's always bothered me about religion." He grinned. "Wonder what the chaplain would have to say about that?"

Jessie covered his cold hand in hers. "He would probably say there are many things we aren't supposed to know, that we have to have faith." Albert frowned at the triteness of her answer and she could feel his hand begin to pull away. She tightened her grip and continued, "But I'll tell you what I think. I think of religion as like an insurance company. There are all these religious 'plans' out there—there are Christians, Muslims, Jews, Hindus, Buddhists, and who knows how many others. I believe that when people choose a religion and follow it with kindness and love in their hearts, when they die, they go to Heaven."

"And how is that like insurance?"

"Why, they're *covered.*"

Albert burst out laughing, and just as quickly, his laughter turned to wheezing. As Jessie helped him inside, he said, between breaths, "Better keep that idea between us. I'm pretty sure the chaplain wouldn't approve."

***

Frank speared a blueberry with his last bite of French toast. "That was delicious," Frank said, putting down his fork. "If we were staying here much longer, I'd probably gain twenty pounds." The happy look she had worn for the last hour dropped from her face, and he was sorry for his choice of words. But he might as well finish it, get it out in the open. "Sara, you're going to have to go home eventually. Don't you think it's time to call your father?"

"Why? Why do I have to go back?" It was more a statement

than a question. She rose and started clearing the table. "I could live here with Jessie for a while. I know she'd let me stay. I could get a job doing something in town. I like it here. I don't want to leave."

"I'm not saying you couldn't come back." Frank sighed heavily; he knew he was going to sound like a fuddy-duddy, but he had to say it. "You have to let your father know where you are. He'll be worried."

She continued to clean the dishes and avoided looking at him. "He's not back yet. He doesn't even know I'm not home." Trying to look busy, she dragged the full trash can out of its space between the refrigerator and cabinet, lifted out the plastic garbage bag, tied it, and set it beside the back door.

"Sara, you can't be happy here unless you're happy there."

"What are you talking about? You don't know me, you don't know my life."

"No, I don't. But I think you left Savannah because you were angry at your father, or just angry at life in general. Here, you think you can be happy and maybe you can, but you need to go back and resolve those old issues first."

Sara folded her arms and looked away. In her heart, she knew he was right. She knew she needed to do something, send a message, something. She just needed more time. Her dad would be back in few days. And what if he came back early?

"Plus, you said you have one year of college left, and…"

"I don't care about that. I want to be happy now. I want to have a normal life—now. Is that too much to ask?"

"Normal?" He thought of the scores of people whose lives had intersected his. He didn't know anyone who didn't have some kind of problem, and so many had problems that were without solutions. "But Sara, your life is normal. Everyone on this planet has problems, sorrow, conflict. They all also have moments, even years, of great joy. It just doesn't happen all at the same time. Or in the sequence we want. We're all happy; we're all sad. That's what normal life is. Peaks and valleys, wins and losses."

"I'm not a child. I know life isn't a fairy tale."

"You're absolutely correct. It is not a fairy tale. And I don't mean that you shouldn't expect or search for happiness, but..."

The doorbell interrupted them, and Frank fervently hoped it wasn't Mitch. He wanted to have a serious chat with that young man before Sara saw him again.

"I'll get it," Sara said, grateful for the interruption.

"No. I'll get it." The tone of his voice stopped her, and she stood quietly and listened as he lumbered to the front of the house, his cane making angry taps on the wooden floors.

Burton Roberts was the last person he expected to see when he opened the front door.

"Hello, I hope I haven't caught you at a bad time," the man said. "I wanted to discuss something with you."

Frank saw that he was holding one of Bill's boxes, and, curious, he invited him inside.

"I've had some inquiries about these, and I've done a little research. Can you call your sculptor friend and find out what he needs to get for each piece so that I can price them?"

"Well, certainly." Frank waited. The other man waited. "Oh, you mean call him right now?"

"If that's possible. I don't mean to be pushy, but customers can be fickle. Give them time to think it over and they're gone to the next shop."

"Of course, please have a seat," he said, motioning to the sofa. "I'll go call him now." He walked toward the coffee table where he had been making his calls, but remembered that he'd left the phone in his bedroom while Sara made breakfast. He pivoted and went down the hall, closing the bedroom door behind him.

Burton smiled with satisfaction. He set the wooden box on the couch and quickly walked into the room with the paintings. This was what he had really come to see.

He went straight to the most vibrant canvas, hastily pulled a cell phone from his pocket, and snapped. He inwardly cursed at the clicking noise, but he could hear the man talking on the phone, so he felt safe. Safe enough to photograph two more paintings. He thought he heard something from the next room and peaked in the kitchen. Reassured that he was alone, he slipped the phone into his pants pocket and pulled out a small magnifying glass. He didn't have time to remove the artwork from the walls to check the backs of the canvases for oxidation, the easiest way he knew to tell if they were old. Instead, he used the magnifying glass to look for crackling lines in the paint. As he did, he sniffed each painting, nodding at the scent of oil paint. Now he knew that these were not decades old, nor were they giclée prints—reproductions printed on canvas and then hand-embellished.

The ones that looked like Chagall paintings appeared to be original. Not original Chagalls—he'd been insane to think otherwise—but original in that instead of simply copying a Chagall painting, the artist had taken several known Chagall designs and ideas and created his own works of genius. He was impressed.

Hearing the squeak of the bedroom door opening, he quickly slipped back into the living room.

"My friend would like to know if you have a suggested price," Frank said, entering the room. In the brief phone call, he and Bill agreed to go with whatever Burton Roberts suggested, mostly to make a sale if in fact Roberts was telling the truth, but also to have a reason to return to the gallery and try to learn more about the man.

Burton sighed. Amateurs, he thought. Out loud, he said, "How about we start with $200 apiece and see how it goes? The shop takes forty percent."

"That sounds excellent. I'm sure he would want me to authorize that price," Frank said. He picked up the box and handed it to the man. "I hope you have good luck with them. You have my number still?" When the man nodded, he added, "Good, good. Well then, I guess we're in business."

After Burton left, Frank went back to the kitchen. At first he thought Sara was gone, but then saw her crouching in the empty space where the trash can was kept, her back pressed to the side of the refrigerator.

"What are you doing there?"

Without answering, she awkwardly emerged from her hiding place.

"That was strange," he said. "It was that Burton Roberts from the gallery. He..."

"I know, I heard," Sara interrupted, somewhat breathless. "He didn't see me, because I hid when I heard him. Frank, when you went into the bedroom he was in the art room. I heard him taking pictures. He was taking pictures of the paintings!"

***

Burton Roberts didn't see Jessie's car come up the street, but she saw him. She watched him leave her house, cut through her neighbor's yard and walk briskly toward the alley that separated her back yard from the small parking area behind the gallery. By the time she parked and came through the front door, she had worked herself into a frenzy.

"What was he doing here?" she demanded.

"He said someone might buy one of Bill's boxes," Frank replied cautiously, taken off guard by Jessie's icy tone. "He wanted to know what price to charge."

"And you believed him? *And* you let him in?" She looked around the living room, letting her eyes rest momentarily on the doorway to the lit dining room. "I don't want him ever in my house again," she said emphatically. *"Never."* With that pronouncement, she walked to her bedroom and slammed the door behind her.

Frank stared at the emptiness she left. He was baffled. Should he go to her and apologize? How was Jessie going to feel when she found out that the man had not just been in the house but also had taken photos? He couldn't begin to imagine how she would react to that. He turned to Sara, expecting her to continue Jessie's scolding.

To his bewilderment, she walked over, gently took him by the arm, and led him to the sofa. "She's not mad at you. I think she's, well, afraid. Why don't you sit here and wait for her to come out? I'll go finish cleaning the kitchen. Then I'll get dressed and..."

she glanced at the front door, and continued, "and who knows? You'll think of something. Or Mitch will." She smiled brightly and went into the kitchen, leaving Frank just as confused as before. Both these women were acting so out of character. What was wrong with Jessie, who had always been so calm and predictable? And Sara? Well, Sara was in love, that's what was wrong with her.

His mind was reeling. Too much was going on. He used to be so good at managing projects and problems. Multi-tasking came so easy to him that a couple of his university friends pasted a decal of a juggler on his office door. It wasn't that long ago, was it? He didn't understand how it could feel like just yesterday and at the same time a lifetime ago. He seldom thought about those days, and when he did, he didn't recognize that person.

He knew several men his age who had trouble letting go. They wanted to relive the past, talk about the old times, the job, their fellow workers. Some missed the work, or the glory they felt they had earned. Others were bitter and held on to resentments and the wrongs they perceived had been done to them. Frank didn't understand it. Surprising everyone, Emmie included, he left his office on a Friday afternoon and never looked back. There were a few friends he stayed in touch with, but for the most part, he simply didn't think about it—other than right now.

Where had the years gone? His mind flipped between Sara and Mitch, Jessie and her distress, Bill and his heart attack, Jose at the gas station, Jackson at the diner—and all the deals and secrets that suddenly seemed too heavy to bear. Weariness overwhelmed him, and he searched inside himself, seeking remnants of the energy and intellect and problem-solving of a different man and a different time and place. If only he could draw on those old talents. If he could only focus. One thing at a time. One crisis at a time.

He sat with his face in his hands, telling himself that he would see more clearly if he could shut out everything and see nothing, just think. When he opened his eyes minutes later, what he saw were his brother's riotous, playful paintings peeking from the next room, mocking him as he sat there with no answers.

***

When Hurricane Katrina hit in 2005, the Gulf of Mexico swept over and through levees and flooded 150,000 houses in New Orleans. TV cameras, newspapers, and Internet images documented the pain, frustration, and losses felt by thousands of people in the city. Overnight, the Big Easy became the big disaster. The misery extended throughout the Gulf Coast, leaving towns, homes, and people devastated. Across the Mississippi coast, 65,000 homes were lost to the storm. In total, more than 1,800 people died and property damage was estimated at between 81 to 100 billion dollars.

With a million residents evacuated from New Orleans, what wind, rain, and tidal surge spared became a buffet for others. Looting was rampant, and cameras documented that disaster, too. But not all thefts were caught by cameras or reported on the news.

Many blocks away from the French Quarter and the Ninth

Ward—in evacuated areas mostly safe from floodwaters—enterprising thieves confidently broke locks and smashed windows in some of the city's most affluent homes, secure in the knowledge that no police cruiser would speed to the scene. The National Guard and local police were focused on rescuing lives, not property. Many saw their opportunity and took it. Jake Burton was one of those.

After losing his job in Los Angeles, Burton headed home to New Orleans. There, he crashed with old friends until he was back on his feet, which didn't take long for a man like him. He was skilled at impressing prospective employers in New Orleans' art district with his knowledge of current and classic artists and their works. He had an art history degree from Xavier University and references from two L.A. galleries. The degree was easily verified, and the two references Burton provided were so positive that his prospective employer didn't bother to find a correct number for the last job listed on his resume, taking him at his word that he was just homesick for his beloved New Orleans.

Burton's luck held. The first month into his new job, and two months before Katrina, he made a major sale for his new employer: a small signed Chagall original color lithograph for $65,000. The gallery owner was so thrilled that he insisted that he and Burton deliver and hang the artwork themselves. With a sizeable commission forthcoming on his next paycheck, Burton was elated. He foresaw prosperity in his new job and for a brief time thought he could make enough money to keep temptation at bay—until he walked through the door of his customer's mansion. The house was filled with dozens of exquisite and diverse pieces, from Warhol pop art to Remington cowboys to glowing

Chihuly glass. And now a *second* Chagall to pair with the one already there! It was more than one person should have, he thought.

Burton actually enjoyed selling to customers who were so enraptured by a piece of art that they would sacrifice in order to have it. How many times had he pretended not to hear as couples whispered or argued about how they would manage to pay for a painting or sculpture? But he never liked collectors. How could they appreciate the beauty of one piece if they had twenty more?

So while he said all the right things to his customer and his employer, Jake Burton helped hang and light the prized lithograph, and wondered how he was going to steal it.

He got his answer weeks later, when he heard the TV anchorman announce that New Orleans was to undergo a mass evacuation due to the oncoming storm. As he helped his employer board up windows and secure the store, Jake told him he was driving an elderly aunt to stay with relatives in Texas. The city was in chaos, and reportedly a million people were either leaving or trying to leave. His boss, who was packing his own SUV with his most valuable inventory, just nodded and left to meet his family and get away before the hurricane hit.

They drove away simultaneously, but Jake circled back, let himself in, picked up an armload of select items, left, and relocked the door. Then he pulled off the boards he had just nailed up and smashed a window to make it look like there had been a burglary. Minutes later, he picked up a friend. Before they joined the exodus from New Orleans, the two men broke into three pricey homes abandoned by their owners, including, of course, the one with the newly acquired Chagall lithograph.

There was no speedy getaway, but then, no one was chasing

them. They were just two people among thousands threading their way north in the pelting rain. As they drove, the men talked of the old days in art classes, the reality of trying to make a living in the art world, and most importantly, their scheme to sell the merchandise hidden under the piles of clothes behind them.

***

When Jessie finally came out of her bedroom, she found Frank sitting in the living room, head in his hands. Her first thought was satisfaction: he deserved to feel bad. Her second thought was remorse for her outburst. She sat down beside him, her anger gone. She couldn't stay mad at him. After all, hadn't she done the same thing herself when she let Burton walk right past her into her house?

"Francis." He looked up, and her heart broke at the misery in his eyes. "I am so sorry I spoke to you the way I did. I over-reacted and lost my temper."

His face relaxed a little. "I'm sorry too, Jessie. I just wasn't thinking. This whole thing has me unsettled and not thinking straight. But I know we can figure it out if we keep at it." He paused. "Unless you think we've all over-reacted and we should just put it out of our minds? I could, uh, take Sara and go back to Knoxville."

"Absolutely not!"

"You're sure?"

"I'm sure."

Standing in the hallway, Sara let out a sigh of relief. Jessie turned to look at her and smiled sheepishly. "You can come out now. I'm through biting people's heads off."

Frank grimaced, knowing too well that Sara's concern didn't lie with Jessie's temperament. But that would have to take a back seat for the moment. He stood up. "Jessie, do you know if Karen has talked to Marilyn yet? Maybe she's learned something. Just one important piece added to what we already have, and I feel sure it will start to make some sense."

"What we already have? I didn't think we had anything," she replied. "But I'll call her right now." She went back to her bedroom to call Karen.

Frank walked into the dining room and stood staring. "What was it in here that caught Burton's attention? What brought him back?"

Sara went to his side, and after looking around to be sure Jessie was still out of earshot, she whispered, "He took three pictures."

"Go on."

"He had time to take more before you came back into the room. But he stopped at three. Could that mean something?"

Simultaneously they turned to the walls, looking for some common denominator that would link three pieces, some clue to explain Burton's interest in Jessie's house. Whatever it was, it was in this room and in three of Tony's paintings.

They were still staring at the artwork when Jessie came in. "Karen had coffee with Marilyn, and she's coming over now to tell us what she found out."

"Good. We'll have another meeting and put our heads together. Sara, would you mind bringing a kitchen chair in here? Maybe it would be helpful to meet in this room."

She frowned. "We should wait for Mitch."

Frank nodded, hiding his irritation. "Yes, but he's probably working now. His mother can call him when she gets here." He sat down heavily in the brown suede and waited.

It was just a matter of minutes before Karen arrived. "Jess, I need a pit stop first," she said, tossing her car keys on the sofa and narrowly missing Gracie. The cat raised her head, glowered, and resumed her nap, pointedly bringing one paw over to cover her eyes. When Karen returned from the bathroom, she found them sitting solemnly around the coffee table. "It took me three cups of caffeine before I could steer the conversation over to those gallery men," she explained. "That is one talkative woman." At their silence, she looked from one solemn face to another. "What? Has something else happened?"

Jessie and Sara turned to Frank. "Burton Roberts came by this morning while you two were at the hospice. He brought by one of the wooden boxes I'd left with him to sell for my friend Bill. Supposedly he was here to talk to me and get a price. But while I was on the phone in the bedroom talking to Bill..." he turned his eyes to Jessie, "he came into this room and took photographs." Jessie sucked in her breath but said nothing. "Sara was in the kitchen where he couldn't see her, but she heard the camera, or maybe cell phone, and believes he took three pictures.

"I am sorry, Jessie; I know that disturbs you—as it does all of us. But it could be just the clue we need."

"What do you mean?" Karen asked. "How is that a clue?"

"Think about it. He brought a camera with him, meaning the

box pricing was a ruse. Even if it were his phone and not a camera, he was so quick about it, he must have come over with that purpose. He would have been rushed for time, knowing I might be back any second. Yet he took three photos, not one. As it turned out, he had more time than he expected, but he didn't take more. That would indicate—as Sara so cleverly deduced—that his interest lies in three of these paintings. Of course, it could be totally innocent. Perhaps he was just photographing his favorites for his own pleasure. But we know that's unlikely. I think he wanted to study them for some reason, or wanted to show these pictures to someone else, maybe his partner." Gesturing across the walls, he said, "If you look for a shared quality among all these, you'll only find common ground among these three." Taking his cane, he pointed to three modernistic and wildly colorful paintings.

The women looked from one painting to the other, saying nothing. Frank waited. He found their silence unsettling. He *had* to be right. There was no other explanation. Burton Roberts was interested in those three peculiar paintings. He couldn't guess why... unless...

"Jessie, do you remember what his reaction was when he came in here that first time? Do you recall what he said?"

"Hmm. I don't know. He didn't say much, but he was definitely impressed." Her mind flew to her late husband and she filled with pride. "Anthony would have been flattered. I remember that man asking if he was a collector, for heaven's sake."

Frank's heart skipped a beat. "What did you say?"

"I *said* he asked if my husband was an artist or a collector," she repeated impatiently. "Is your hearing going as well as your knees?"

"I meant, what did you say in reply to him?"

"I probably told him both. You know Anthony bartered some of his works with a couple of art professors over at UT. So that made him a collector." Jessie slowly began to understand. "Oh, that's just ridiculous. You think he thinks those are original masterpieces?"

"I don't know, but I do believe he wants them," said Frank. Seeing the skepticism on their faces, he added, "It's not common, but occasionally a painting pops up out of the blue. You hear about some lucky soul buying a Picasso for six dollars at a garage sale. Or a painting gets stolen, hidden, and then reappears years later. It could be that our man took the photos so he could try to find them in a listing somewhere and see their value, and maybe try to buy them from you, Jessie. Or maybe his motives aren't so honest."

"I think we need to call Mitch," Sara said.

Karen agreed, albeit reluctantly. She wondered if these gallery men were dangerous. Would they hurt someone over a piece of art? She suddenly wished her youngest son had chosen a different profession. Although she was proud of him for being a deputy, she never before thought he would be at risk, not here living and working in Deer Creek. Now she knew she'd never feel the same. There was no truly safe place. Greed made people crazy.

Jessie disrupted her thoughts. "Karen, did you learn anything from Marilyn?"

"Not much. She said the one named Burton is from New Orleans. He told her he'd worked at galleries in Los Angeles and then opened his own place in New Orleans. He said he lost it to Katrina and was starting over when he came here." Remembering Marilyn's animated conversation, she added, "And she said he flirted with her."

"Excellent!" Frank's booming voice startled the women. "This gives us something solid to look into," he explained. "It shouldn't be hard to find out if Burton Roberts had a place in New Orleans and if it was damaged by Katrina. Although I'd bet good money he lied. But we can find out soon enough."

He turned his attention back to the paintings. "Jess, dear, do you remember anything about these three pieces? For instance, did Tony copy these from prints like he did sometimes, or were they his own creations?"

As Jessie and Frank fell into conversation about the paintings, Karen and Sara exchanged looks. He had just called Jessie "dear." Sara thought it was sweet. Karen wondered if her friend had even noticed, and if so, what thoughts were dancing around behind those serious eyes. A romantic, she often thought the two older people would make a nice couple. Then they wouldn't be alone. But when she mentioned it once to her, Jessie just laughed and told her she was too old to start over.

She heard her son's name and returned her focus to their conversation. They were asking her when Mitch would be around.

"He called me right after he got to work this morning, and said he had to go somewhere today for the sheriff. I don't know what time he'll be back," Karen said.

Frank thought a minute, unconsciously rubbing his hand over his knee. "Jessie, we should pay Burton Roberts another visit. How would you feel about telling him you've reconsidered exhibiting Tony's pictures?" He held up his hand when she started to protest. "I'm not saying we'd ever get to that point, okay? But we need to throw him off balance—make him think we trust him, or at the very least, not let him know we don't trust him. Do you think you can do that?"

Jessie chewed on her bottom lip, her whole face in a scowl. "I can't live like this," she finally said, "being afraid in my own home, worried about what I don't know and can't see. I've got to do something about it. And if that means being nice to that man to trick him, I'll try. Do you have a plan?"

"Not exactly... yet."

"Well then, we'll just jump off that bridge when we get to it."

***

Mitch was annoyed. Driving to Nashville to run errands for the sheriff was not how he had envisioned spending the day. That morning, Sheriff Duggan had given him an address and a name and told him to pick up a package and bring it directly back to him. He didn't say what it was or why it couldn't be shipped. He usually wasn't so mysterious, Mitch reflected. But deputies quickly learn not to complain to the sheriff, and in the last couple of days, Mitch had the impression he had somehow gotten on his boss's bad side. He couldn't explain it, but he felt like the sheriff was watching him, waiting for him to do something wrong.

Bored by the monotony of interstate driving, he picked up his cell phone and pressed a shortcut key to make a call.

After two rings, Karen answered. "We were just talking about you," she said.

"Who's we?"

"I'm at Jessie's. You won't believe what's happened now."

"You're at Jessie's? Is Sara there?"

"Well, yes."

"Would you put her on?"

Karen hesitated for a moment, her face frozen; then she held her cell out to Sara. "Mitch wants to talk to you."

Sara stood, took the phone, and walked toward the window, facing away from the trio as she tried to hide both the flush she felt coming on her face and her pleasure that Mitch had asked for her. "Hi."

"Hey there. I'm sorry, but it doesn't look like I'll be around there today. I'm just outside of Nashville. The sheriff sent me here this morning to pick up a package. Maybe evidence or something. He made it sound like it was too important to be mailed. I don't know when I'll be back, but if it's not too late, would you like to grab some dinner?"

"Sure, that sounds great. Just stop by whenever you get back. Things have been happening here, and I know everyone will want to talk to you."

"What happened?

"That man from the art gallery came over this morning and he took pictures of some of the paintings while Frank was in the bedroom. He was being real sneaky about it. Now your mom was just telling us what she found out from the real estate lady. Here, I'll let her tell you… I…I'll see you tonight." Smiling, she handed the phone back to Karen and sat down again.

As Karen talked quietly to her son, Sara glanced at Frank and Jessie and saw the looks passing between them. "What?" she asked.

A humph sound came from Frank, while Jessie innocently asked when Mitch would be coming over.

***

Arriving in Nashville, Mitch followed the directions on the slip of paper Sheriff Duggan had given him. After several blocks, he parked and reread the directions. Certain that he'd made a wrong turn somewhere, he retraced his steps and got back to the I-40 exit that he had taken. After following the directions again, he pulled into a parking lot and called the dispatcher in Deer Creek.

"It's Mitch. Is the sheriff there? I need to talk to him. He sent me to Nashville to pick up something, but the directions he gave me seem to be wrong." He waited while the dispatcher checked, only to be told that the sheriff was in a meeting and said to call back in an hour.

Mitch hung up and drummed his fingers on the steering wheel. Annoyed, he checked his watch, then put the car into gear and drove west of downtown, deciding if he was going to cool his heels waiting, at least he would get some enjoyment from it. Ten minutes later, he stood gazing up at a 42-foot tall statue of the goddess Athena.

Centennial Park and its Parthenon—a full-scale reproduction of the ancient Parthenon—was one of his favorite spots in Nashville, mostly because of the sculpture that dominated it. A replica of the famous ivory, gold, and silver statue from ancient Greece, Nashville's Athena Parthenos stood in gold-leaf splendor, as enigmatic today as she must have been in old Athens. He was no expert on Greek mythology, but he never tired of seeing Athena—the sphinx on her helmet, Medusa on her breast, the six-foot statute of Victory, or Nike, in her right hand, and a shield and spear on her left.

To the average tourist, the 46-column building and gilded statue might seem odd in a city known for country music, but long before the Grand Ole Opry, Nashville's refinement, colleges, and public school system had earned it the nickname *Athens of the South*. Although its wealth and refinement were devastated by the Civil War, the city rebuilt itself afterwards, and as a monument to its culture, built their Parthenon in 1897 as part of the Tennessee Centennial Exposition, adding Athena almost a century later.

As Mitch gazed up at the exotic face, he imagined it with blue hair and piercings. For the thousandth time that week, he thought of Sara. He grinned, recalling the previous night, their long talk, and the electricity he felt when he kissed her. He wondered what she was doing right now, at Jessie's house. His grin disappeared as he recalled how upset Jessie and Frank had been last night. He wanted to help. Athena gave her shrewd aid to mythical heroes such as Odysseus, Jason, and Heracles. Mitch knew he was no hero, but with Sara by his side, maybe he could do something. He looked gravely at the huge statue. Who was he kidding? Heroic powers were mythical. He and Sara were just people. But people drew strength from each other. He couldn't explain what he was feeling. Was it love? He barely knew her. Still, he felt that with Sara by his side, he could do... What? Anything? No, he was too much of a pragmatist to believe that.

But standing here just thinking of her, he felt different, stronger. He almost laughed out loud at his thoughts. Maybe there was something to the Athena story after all.

Just then, a cell phone ring broke the silence around him and he automatically turned toward its sound. A well-dressed man coming from another room pulled a phone from his blazer pocket and frowned at the I.D. screen before answering. There was something oddly familiar about him, and Mitch thought maybe the man was a musician whose face he had seen on TV or on an album cover. As Mitch tried to place him, the man looked up, sensing someone watching him. It was only a couple of seconds, but Mitch was sure he saw puzzlement and recognition in the stranger's face. The man turned quickly and rapidly walked away, and as he did, Mitch saw the gray pony-tail.

***

Frank finally stopped tapping his cane. "Why don't the four of us go over there now? It's time we turned the tables on him. He's been here twice—uninvited—and made us uncomfortable. Let's do the same. We'll put some pressure on him by hanging around there and looking at his inventory and asking questions. If he's legitimate, and if we ask enough questions, he's bound to give us some answers. That's really what we're trying to find out. Answers. Is he an honest merchant or is something fishy going on? It could be that he's just an odd bird. But if he's not a legitimate art dealer, then maybe his inventory isn't legitimate either. Jessie, if you can keep him occupied talking about Tony's paintings, the rest of us can find the most expensive pieces and memorize as much as we can about them. Then we can come back and research the artists and see if we can learn anything about them."

"What's that going to tell us? And why the most expensive pieces?" asked Jessie.

"Because those would be the ones whose artists we'd be more likely to find on the Internet."

"Oh." Her confusion lifted and her eyes widened. "Do you really believe that the paintings in the gallery are stolen?"

"That's one possibility. If even just one was stolen, it might turn up in a news story somewhere. Or maybe we can find an email address for one of the artists. Then I could contact him, or her, and ask about this Burton guy. I know it's a long shot, but what have we got to lose? At least we'll be doing something instead of sitting here worrying. If we find that one was stolen, that would give us the proof we need to go to the sheriff."

The women nodded their agreement, Jessie adding, "God help me, I hope I can talk to that man without letting him see how I really feel. He gives me the creeps."

***

Two blocks from Centennial Park, the pony-tailed stranger was trying not to shout into his cell phone. "I don't care how you do it, but get rid of him. We can't afford to screw up this deal," he said. He listened for a moment, then, shaking his head in disgust, he interrupted the voice on the other end. "I thought you had this under control... Just take care of it. I'm on my way there now."

***

Following their plan, Sara and Karen entered the gallery. Burton Roberts was behind the counter, talking to a thin, nervous-looking man who was jangling car keys in his hand.

"Hello, ladies." Recognizing Sara, he smiled and added, "Welcome back. Let me know if I can help you with anything." The women gave their hellos and began browsing the shop, glancing back repeatedly at the men behind the counter. Five minutes later, the door chimed and Frank and Jessie walked in. Again Burton looked up and welcomed the customers. His associate, still silent, shoved the keys into his pocket and busied himself wiping imaginary dust off the counter with his hands. Jessie surprised them both by walking directly to them and plopping her handbag on the counter.

"I've been thinking about your offer," she said, her voice a little too loud.

"Yes?"

"The exhibit," she said, trying to calm herself and not sound nervous. "Do you still want to display the paintings?"

Burton stared at her in surprise, his face slowly forming a genuine smile. "Oh yes, Mrs. Cunningham. We would be thrilled to have them."

"All right then," she said. "How do we go about this? I mean, which ones do you want to show, and for how long, and where would you put them? And, you'll take good care of them, won't you? Do I need to fill out any paperwork?" All the questions they had planned for her to ask to tie up his time came out in a tumble, and she wondered how long she could keep him distracted. She hoped the others could work fast.

She needn't worry. Burton was totally focused on her, and Harris was just as focused on their conversation.

"You don't know how happy I am to hear that," Burton said. "What I was hoping was to exhibit the three that look like Chagall paintings. They're exquisite."

Jessie blinked. "Chagall?"

"Yes," replied Burton. "The first time I saw them, I was spellbound. They looked so much like his work. I took another peek at them yesterday when I stopped by to see your friend there." He nodded toward Frank. "And looking at them again, I saw them for what they are. Not copies, but originals. Your husband painted them, right?" He paused as she gave a slight nod. "He was brilliant. He captured the style and imagination of Chagall but the paintings are his own unique work. Very much like students would study a master artist, imitate his style, and then develop their own works."

Jessie was having a hard time following him. Again, all she could say was, "Chagall?"

Burton smiled indulgently at her. "Here, I'll show you the three we'd like to exhibit." He pulled his cell phone from his pants pocket, tapped a few keys, and angled the phone so that Jessie could see as he scrolled through the photos taken at her house.

"I snapped these so that I could show Harris here. He agrees with me that they are just phenomenal. It's almost a crime not to share them with your community."

A strange noise came from the previously silent partner. Harris's hand covered his mouth as he coughed said, "Yes, ma'am. It'd be a crime."

"If you'd like, we can set up the exhibit tomorrow morning," Burton added. "People are just starting to drop in and see what we're all about. So the sooner the better. Now's the best time to have the most eyes on the paintings."

By this time, Jessie's friends had stopped their surreptitious survey of the gallery's works and were looking at one another, confused by the man's candidness. Frank, the first to recover, stepped over to Jessie's side. "Didn't you say you were working tomorrow, Jessie?"

She sensed a caution in his voice and understood his cue. Turning to Burton, she said, "Actually, I'm not available tomorrow. I'm a volunteer at the hospice a couple days a week… not that I'm there all day, but I would like to be here when you hang the pictures. I would just feel more comfortable watching."

"Certainly, I understand that," said Burton. "Just let us know when you are free. We'll accommodate your schedule. But like I said, the sooner the better."

Frank moved closer to Burton and started a conversation about Bill's wooden boxes while Jessie drifted to one of the display panels. As she did, Harris walked over to her. Almost whispering, he asked, "You say you work at a hospice? Here in town?"

The man was skin and bones, she realized. Seeing the dark half-circles under his eyes and the looseness of his clothes, Jessie wondered if he was ill. As sympathy overcame suspicion, her distrust faded and she began talking about the hospice, softly answering his questions and describing the facility, its staff, and schedules in detail.

Ten minutes later, Frank interrupted them and asked Jessie if she was ready to leave.

From across the room, Karen glanced at her watch and said, "Oh look at the time. We need to be going, too. You ready, Sara?"

As they filed out of the shop, Frank and Jessie went left and Karen and Sara went right. As Karen looked into her purse for her car key, she bumped into a man on the sidewalk.

"Excuse…" she started, but abruptly stopped. The man, someone she had never seen before, was looking at her quizzically.

"My fault. Sorry," he said, staring at her and seeming to want to say more. Instead, he turned and quickly walked into the gallery.

She watched him go inside, wondering who he was, and then hurried to catch up with Sara—unaware that the stranger had been watching her and Sara through the front display window as they discreetly scribbled on slips of paper and hid them in their pockets.

***

"Now what?" It was more a statement than a question, and although it was Jessie who spoke, it seemed to sum up what they were all thinking.

"I don't know. I just don't know." Frank was as puzzled as the others. "He was so open about taking the pictures. There didn't appear to be anything underhanded or deceitful about it. I *guess* we could have misjudged these men. Perhaps all of this has just been coincidence and imagination." Even as he said it he didn't believe it. The newspaper ad simply made no sense. "Still, it wouldn't hurt to go on with our plan and check out the artists whose paintings he has."

"My computer is ready now," Karen said, bringing a laptop to her kitchen table where they gathered. At Jessie's insistence, she relinquished dinner duty to her and for the next hour took turns with Sara typing in artist names and painting titles while Frank made suggestions and took notes.

Jessie took over Karen's kitchen and made omelets for them, and then sat quietly, exhausted from the day's events. More so, the man's praise for the paintings had stirred up memories, and the emotional jog took its toll. Her heart was no longer in their investigation. She was tired and wanted to retreat to her house, to the rooms that had been so silent since her husband's death. She said nothing, just watched and listened while the others worked.

Their Internet search turned up little, mostly web pages on the artists and gallery phone numbers where paintings could be bought. There were no references to thefts or artwork lost in Katrina. There were no links to New Orleans galleries. There were no references to Burton Roberts.

Karen had just closed her laptop when her cell rang. She glanced at the caller ID and answered, "Hi, honey, where are you?" She listened for a minute, said goodbye, and stoically handed the phone to Sara. "He has to stay in Nashville overnight," she said to the others. Sara spoke softly into the phone as she turned her back to the others and walked out of the kitchen.

"As soon as she's off the phone, I think we should go home," said Jessie. "I'm really tired."

Frank and Karen murmured their agreement and immediately began tidying up the table. "We'll regroup tomorrow," he said. "Maybe overnight one of us will have an epiphany."

Jessie frowned, weary of the intrigue. "I wish they'd just pack up and leave."

8. SATURDAY

Sleep eluded Frank most of the night, which wasn't altogether unusual. The older he got, the less he slept. He frequently woke up every two hours, his mind racing from one idea to another. Last night was worse than usual, and when he glimpsed the dawn, he gave up and got up.

As he put on yesterday's clothes, he yearned to be in his own home again. He had never liked living out of a suitcase. He thought of the Ben Franklin line about guests and fish after three days and wondered if his sister-in-law was ready for them to leave. When he walked into the kitchen to make coffee, he was stunned to see Jessie and Sara sitting at the table. He wasn't sure, but the bowls beside Jessie's coffee cup looked to have traces of chocolate ice-cream. Their contented smiles told him that old Ben would have been wrong about this house.

"This is a surprise. You two are up awfully early."

"Good morning. I was just telling Sara about a dream I had last night," said Jessie. "It was so peculiar. It was like I was in a science fiction world, and in that world, each person got one do-over in their life. Isn't that interesting?"

Frank's eyebrows went up. "What a strange dream. Whatever were you thinking about when you went to bed last night that made you dream that?"

"I don't recall thinking about anything. I was dead tired last night. I went right to sleep." She looked at her houseguests thoughtfully and said, "But it is an interesting idea, don't you think?"

Sara nodded. "I know one thing I would certainly do over."

Jessie smiled with affection at the girl, intuitively knowing what she was thinking. "Yes, but then you would never have come here, would you?"

"You're right, I would never have met you or Frank…or Mitch. I guess things have a way of working out."

Frank started to object but stopped. Instead, he fixed his coffee and sat down with the women, thinking there were innumerable events he would change if he had the power. But such power, he thought, came only in a silly dream; the reality is that you have limited control over what happens in your or other people's lives, and you often just have to make the best of it. He swallowed his thoughts with his coffee. It was too early for philosophy. "A do-over, huh? That could get complicated."

"Ooh, yes," said Jessie. "Even as I dreamed it, I could see how messy it could get. One action undone could affect someone else's actions and so on and so on. But wouldn't it be something if we really did have the power to change things, instead of having to make the best of what comes our way?"

It was as if she had read his mind, and not for the first time. Frank shifted in his chair, uneasy with the thought.

"Well, I'd best get ready for hospice," said Jessie. "I will be glad when my schedule gets back to normal." Seeing the expressions on their faces, she quickly added, "I don't mean you two, I mean the other volunteer whose schedule I've been working this week. She's been out sick."

"Is there anything you want me to do for you today?" asked Sara.

"No, dear. You've already done so much for me this week. The house positively sparkles, it's so clean. And that reminds me, Sara, I haven't forgotten your money. I'll stop at the bank this morning before they close and get some cash out so that I can pay you."

Sara's face reddened. "I wasn't hinting at that. I don't even care about the money. I've enjoyed every minute here, really, I have."

"Not as much as I have. But a deal is a deal. So don't even think of arguing with me." She reached over and patted Sara on the head. "You're a delight to have around." She picked up a lock of hair and added, "Why don't you take the day off, take a bubble bath, just relax today."

Sara laughed. "You know the blue isn't going to wash out. But I can take a hint. I'll get cleaned up."

Frank stared as Sara, still laughing, got up and left the kitchen. He almost missed the sullen girl who shrank from anyone's touch. As soon as she was out of earshot, he turned abruptly to Jessie. "What are we going to do about Mitch and Sara?"

"What do you mean? What about them?"

"You know what I mean."

"No, I don't. Mitchell is a nice boy, and Sara is a nice girl. She just dances to her own drummer. There's nothing to be 'done' about them."

"There's something going on between them, and I don't like it."

"Francis, you're always trying to change people. Just let them be. Not everyone can be changed, or even understood—and not everyone should see the world from your point of view. How boring it would be if everyone was just alike."

"Is that what you think," he sputtered, "that I try to change people? I would never presume to do that."

"Well, isn't that what you're doing?"

"I..." He stopped, frustrated and almost angry. They sat silently for a minute, both unexpectedly uncomfortable.

Jessie broke first. "Oh Francis, I don't want to argue with you. I know you mean well, and you're the kindest, most generous man I've ever known. Your heart is always in the right place. You just go ahead and do what you think is best." She got up and put her coffee cup in the sink. "I really need to get going now. You'll be all right here?"

"Of course." He paused. "Maybe I am a little controlling."

Jessie's eyes widened. "A little?"

He sighed in reply. "Go get ready. I'll be fine. I have a ton of calls to make this morning, and I'm going to talk to Mitch... about the gallery, not Sara."

***

"Thanks, Sis. I appreciate you putting me up for the night. Yesterday was the strangest day ever. I've never known the sheriff to be so inefficient. But I guess even he's entitled to a screw-up once in a while."

"No problem. Next time, bring Mom. It would do her good to get out more. She's never going to meet anyone as long as she stays in Deer Creek. I'd say you too, but from what you told me last night, I think you don't need any help." She gave her younger brother a kiss on the cheek and they said goodbye.

As Mitch drove off, he pondered the past 24 hours. The unexpected drive to Nashville. Incorrect directions. The pony-tailed man at the Parthenon. The sheriff's peculiar absence whenever he tried to call. And, when he finally did reach him, instructions to stay overnight and pick up the package at—of all places—the Vanderbilt library. He didn't understand it, but then, he didn't have to. He just had to get the package back to the sheriff—and quickly, he hoped. He had other things to do today.

An hour later, he was back on the phone with the dispatcher. "Can't you reach him? He specifically told me that the package I'm supposed to pick up for him was being held for me at the Vanderbilt Library, main desk." He listened for a moment, then interrupted the dispatcher. "There are *eight* libraries here, and I've already been to the main library and one other and they don't know what I'm talking about. Frankly, I'm beginning to wonder myself. I don't even know what it is that I'm supposed to be picking up. Look, just please try to reach him and tell him to call me right away. Meanwhile, I'll do what I can here."

After another hour of driving around the campus, parking, walking, and talking to the four more librarians, all of them inexplicably amused, he finally had the package in his hands. "The Divinity Library," he muttered to himself, turning the thick brown envelope in his hands. "What on earth is in here?"

***

Alice frowned when she saw Jessie. The older woman looked extraordinarily tired, almost fragile, as though the slightest difficulty would crush her, both in body and spirit. Although Alice usually paid little attention to the volunteers' schedules, she was well aware that they were supposed to limit their days and hours. Not only was she certain that her favorite volunteer had exceeded her limit for the week, but she was also worried about her health.

"How many days have you worked this week?" she asked the woman.

"Good morning, Alice. We're short on volunteers right now." She gave a faint smile, deliberately not answering the question. "We'll all be back on regular hours in a day or two."

"I hope so. I don't want you to over-do it." She paused before returning to her rounds. "We got a couple of new patients late yesterday," she said. She waited until two visitors passed by, and, lowering her voice, added, "Both dementia."

The women shared a sorrowful look. Jessie spoke first, sensing the nurse's reluctance to voice her feelings. "I find these the hardest to help. I don't know if it's because I can't tell if they understand what's happening, or if it's because I'm afraid that one day I'll be in their place."

Alice didn't have to answer; her eyes spoke her understanding. She took Jessie's hand and squeezed it lightly, then walked away.

***

Frank turned the key. Nothing, not even a click this time.

"You need a new battery," Sara said, bending over to talk to him through the open window. "I can't believe you didn't get it replaced before you drove back from Knoxville. You know that's very dangerous, to be on the road in an unreliable car."

Frank bristled. The last thing he wanted to hear was Sara lecturing him. "Jessie will be home shortly. Then I'll borrow her car and go find a battery."

"Where were you going, anyway?" she asked, oblivious to his bad mood.

"I thought I'd go by the newspaper office and talk to Gary again."

"Why?" She glanced around and lowered her voice. "About the gallery? Did you think of something else?"

He looked at her thoughtfully, his annoyance now banished by a new idea. "Maybe. Let's go inside and talk."

When Jessie got home, she found the two of them sitting in the dining room, Frank making notes while Sara pulled up webpages on his smart phone. He looked up at Jessie. "She's much faster at this than I am," he explained. "I'm okay on a computer but don't have the patience to type on my phone."

"Typing on a phone?" she mused. "I am so behind the times. My kids keep telling me I've living in the 20th Century. I guess they're right." She pulled a bank envelope from her purse and handed it to Sara. "Here you go, dearie. Now, what exactly are you two doing?"

Frank put down his pen. "I was thinking about our research last night. We were looking for specific paintings and artists, but maybe what we need first is some general information on art crime. So we googled 'stolen art' and 'art theft' and found a number of web pages describing modern art crime."

"Like what?"

"You wouldn't believe it, Jessie. In addition to lots of outright thefts, there's also a lot of fraud—art forgeries, where people paint exact replicas of valuable old paintings, make them look old, and pass them off as the real thing."

Jessie sat down, shaking her head in disbelief. "Isn't that something. A person has that much talent and uses it that way, instead of building his own career under his own name."

"It's the money, of course. We're talking hundreds of thousands of dollars, sometimes millions," said Frank.

"And then there's the art stolen by the Nazis," added Sara. "You might remember there was a movie about it. Some of that art is sold on the black market."

"Well, yes, but what does any of that have to do with the gallery?" she asked. "None of their paintings are outlandishly expensive, and the artists' names we saw aren't famous. And Nazis? I don't understand where you're going with this."

"I don't know myself," Frank admitted. "But if we keep looking, maybe we'll come across something important. Maybe we'll find a connection to art theft during Katrina or New Orleans or..."

"Or the newspaper code," Sara added.

"That's right," he said. "If we could find a reference to that, then we could take it to the sheriff."

"I don't want to burst your bubble," said Jessie, "but I think we're in over our heads. I think we should get the sheriff over here and tell him what we know, or don't know, and let him go talk to those men. Maybe he could look around upstairs over there and see if they're up to no good."

Frank looked down at his notes. Yes, their research was interesting, and yes, Burton Roberts appeared to be disingenuous. But maybe Jessie was right. They were going in circles and getting nowhere. He sighed. "Okay. When Mitch gets here, we'll go over it all once again and have him call the sheriff. But if the sheriff disagrees and tells us we're off base, are you willing to give it up?"

"If it comes to that, we won't have a choice," Jessie replied, then turned toward a scratching noise coming from the bedrooms. "Did you hear that?" She got up and hurried out of the room. Frank and Sara followed.

"Gracie! Stop that!" But it was too late. Jessie's cat was on the hallway floor on her back, her jaws clamped in a death grip on Frank's hat, her paws in the air, furiously shredding straw. When Jessie attempted to take the hat from her, Gracie flipped over and tried to run into Sara's bedroom. Her exit was hampered by a claw caught in the brim of the hat, resulting in an ungraceful and comical escape.

The three rushed into Sara's room. Jessie was mortified at her cat's destruction. Frank was red-faced with anger. Sara was overcome with helplessness, seeing at once that in the cat's beeline to sanctuary under the bed, the hat she was dragging had toppled Sara's backpack and jeans—both of which she had carefully positioned on the floor to hide her cell phone and charger.

While Jessie coaxed her cat out of hiding and retrieved the ruined hat, Frank picked up the phone and handed it to Sara. "I'm sorry," she said, her voice a whisper. "I didn't mean to lie to you." He took his destroyed hat from Jessie and left the room. Seconds later, she heard the front door open and close.

"What was that all about?" Jessie asked.

"I told him I didn't have a phone."

"Why?"

She hung her head. "When I told him I was stranded and asked him for help, I knew he would expect me to call someone to come get me. I didn't want to go home. And my dad was on the other side of the world and I was too embarrassed to call any of my friends—lately I haven't been much of a friend to them. I didn't know what to do, so I lied. I actually said my phone was run over by a truck. And it was such a stupid lie, because of course I could have used anyone's phone to call home." She wiped tears from her eyes. "What's the matter with me, Jessie? Why do I mess up everything?"

"Oh sweetie, don't talk like that." Jessie put her arms around her and hugged her tightly. "We all mess up from time to time. You haven't done anything that can't be fixed. He'll get over it. He'll even get over that awful old hat. Now let's go find him and clear the air. He's probably sitting on the front porch."

When they opened the front door, he was in fact on the porch, sitting on the glider, wiping perspiration from his forehead.

Before anyone could speak, though, Mitch pulled into the driveway in a squad car. When he saw Sara, he smiled broadly, got out of the car, and walked to the porch.

"Hi. I only have a minute; I haven't been to the office yet. I just wanted to swing by and say hello." The trio on the porch just stared at him. "What's wrong? Did something happen?" He looked at them anxiously. Sara turned and ran into the house. Jessie continued to stare, her eyes narrowing in disapproval.

"I didn't think the day could get more complicated," Frank said.

"What is it? What's wrong?"

Still sitting on the glider, Frank pointed first to a spot on his own cheek and then pointed to Mitch. "Lipstick."

"What?"

"There's lipstick on your face."

The deputy rubbed his hand over his cheek and looked with amusement at the red stain on his hand. "So that's why people were staring at me this morning." He looked from Frank to Jessie, realization setting in. "Oh for God's sake, it's from my *sister.* I got stuck in Nashville last night and stayed at her place. She kissed me goodbye this morning." He waited for their reply, but neither said anything. Tired and frustrated from the past 24 hours, he shoved his hands in his pockets. "Look, I have to go. I shouldn't even have taken the time to stop here first." With that, he left the porch and walked back to the car. As he opened the door, he turned back to them. "Tell Sara that if she wants to see me, she knows where to find me."

After his car was gone, Jessie walked over and sat down beside Frank. "Oh dear. He's right to be annoyed with us. How could we jump to conclusions like that? We're all showing our bad sides. *All* of us." She patted his hand. "She made a mistake about the phone. It was just a mistake, not who she is. You know that. Come on, come back inside out of this heat."

He got up first, steadying the glider for her. "Okay. Let's go straighten out this mess. And Jessie," he said, "for the record, I loved that hat."

***

By the time they came inside, Sara had already packed her things and had taken them to the living room. They found her in the bedroom, sitting on the side of the bed, cell phone in her hand.

"I'm ready to go home," she said.

Frank sighed. "As it just so happens, I am, too."

"Oh no you don't," Jessie interjected, her hands on her hips. "You two can't leave now. Sara, you need to go find Mitchell right now and apologize to him. Yes, that's what I said, apologize. The lipstick you saw was from his sister. You didn't give him a chance to explain; you just ran off." Her voice turned softer and she clasped her hands together. "My dear, it's time to start running toward things, not away from them.

"And you, Frank, you can't leave until we talk to the sheriff, like you said we would. Today. Then if you want to leave tomorrow, that will be fine. I'll be fine."

Would she be fine? None of them were sure.

***

After much debate, Jessie and Sara agreed to take her car to go find Mitch. A face-to-face apology was better than a phone call. Frank needed to stay and make calls of his own—the first being to locate a battery for his car.

"Sara, take your phone with you and I'll call when I find a

battery. You can stop on the way home and pick it up. I can put it in myself," he said, adding, "or maybe get Mitch to help me." Reminded of Sara's cell phone, he thought of how normal it was now for people to be on their phones constantly, even an old coot like him. Either Sara had a lot of self-control, to be able to stay off her phone for days, or her strange fabrication was caused by desperation. Maybe both.

"What's your number?"

Sara picked up a piece of junk mail off the table, scribbled her number in the margin, and gave it to him on their way out the door.

It took longer to find Jessie's phone book on top of the refrigerator than it did to locate a parts store that had the battery. He reached for the paper where Sara had written her cell number. He smiled at her writing. Instead of turning the paper and writing the number perpendicular to the printing, she'd written parallel, stacking the numbers: area code on one line, the next three numbers underneath, the final four numbers on the next line, followed by a smiley face.

His grin disappeared. The scribbled numbers reminded him of something else. Something important. He struggled to remember. Suddenly, he jumped from the chair and hurried to his bedroom and began rummaging through his bag. Quickly he found what he was searching for. He opened the envelope and pulled out the newspaper ad. He read it again, this time focusing on the numbers.

"Manager. Deer Creek Nature Preserve. Immediate opening for supervisor of 504-acre sanctuary. Must have degrees in Botany and Wildlife Management. 12 years' experience required. Typical re-

location package. P.O. Box 64876, Deer Creek, TN. Attn: Charles Gallager."

Following the improvised format Sara had used, he wrote down the numbers on the envelope:

504

126

4876

His heart was racing. He reread the ad again and the words and numbers seemed to pop out: 504-126-4876, relocation package, Deer Creek, TN. What was he missing? There had to be more of a message. Carefully he read the ad over and over, trying to see a double meaning or a sequence of letters that might spell something. He could call the number and see who answered. But that would mean he'd be giving his number and probably his identity to whomever answered—if it were really a phone number. He read the ad once more. Gallager. Maybe there was a Charles Gallager in the phone book. It was worth a try. He turned to the G's. Nothing.

Again he looked at the numbers he'd written. This time he turned to the front of the phone book, looking for a map that showed zip codes.

Slowly he closed the phone book and picked up his phone and Sara's number, ready to forget the battery and call her and Jessie to come home. After punching in three numbers, he hung up and put down the phone. He turned over the paper and again began writing, this time randomly choosing letters from words in the newspaper ad. After several tries, he gasped. As he turned and stared into the dining room, the paper fell from his hand and fluttered to the floor.

9. SATURDAY AFTERNOON

The station was oddly deserted when he walked in, with only the dispatcher in sight. Although Mitch usually stopped to say hello and see what was happening, today he ignored him and walked straight back to Sheriff Dave Duggan's corner office. The cool reception he'd gotten at Jessie's had thrown him for a loop and he was in no mood for chitchat. Seeing the sheriff alone at his desk, he knocked on the open door and carefully placed the package in front of him. He stood mutely, waiting.

"What's this?"

Mitch bit back a retort and silently counted to ten.

"Oh. The evidence package from Nashville. Thanks," he said, moving the package to the top of his In-tray.

Mitch tried counting to ten again, but this time only made it to three. "*That's it?*"

The sheriff's eyes narrowed. "You want a medal? I said thanks."

"Sorry, sir." He tried hard to hide the irritation from his face and voice. "What I meant to say was, do you need me for anything else?"

"No, that's all." For a few seconds they stared awkwardly at one another, each expecting the other to speak. Instead, a few tinny bars of Mozart played from the sheriff's pocket. He pulled out his cell phone, answering with, "Just a minute." He looked at Mitch and said, "Close the door on your way out."

Mitch was on the sidewalk fuming when a familiar voice stopped him. "Hey, Officer, I want to file a complaint."

He turned. "Ali. What are you doing here?"

"Well. I'm glad to see you, too." She gave him her best flirty look, undeterred by his lack of enthusiasm. "I saw you rush in a few minutes ago and tried to catch you then. You must be working on something important."

"No, just busy and not having a very good day." He paused. "What's new with you?"

"Nothing much, I just thought maybe you'd like to get together sometime. It's been a while." When he didn't respond, she sighed. "It's that girl I saw you with the other day, isn't it?" She shrugged her shoulders. "I thought so. It's okay. Not a big deal. Really." He still didn't respond. "*Really*," she said, this time her smile genuine. "Mitch, we've been friends since grade school. We'll always be friends." She softly brushed her fingers across his cropped hair. "Just don't get carried away and dye yours blue, too."

Although uncomfortable with her gesture, he was strangely relieved at her words. It felt good, no, it felt *right,* to have someone recognize his feelings. He took a deep breath and let a smile slide across his face. "Thanks Ali," he said. "I don't know what's going to..." He stopped in mid-sentence, seeing over her shoulder a figure watching them from across the parking lot.

Ali looked back in time to see Sara spin around and walk away.

"I've got to go," Mitch said quickly, but before he could move, a squad car pulled up to the curb and another deputy leaned out the window.

"Hey man, where were you today? You missed all the excitement. There was a robbery over at that nursing home and somebody got clobbered." The deputy in the car lowered his voice and said, "Wherever you were, I'm glad, 'cause since you weren't around, they called me, and this is the most action I've seen since I took this job." He winked at Ali and drove off.

Mitch looked over to where Sara had been standing, but she was now gone. He was confused. He wondered why the sheriff hadn't said anything to him about a robbery.

"What nursing home?" Ali asked. "Did he mean the hospice?"

His face paled. "Mom works there."

"Go!" she said, as he turned and rushed back inside.

He reached the dispatcher just as he got off a call. "Did something happen at the hospice today?"

The dispatcher looked up at him over his glasses. "You just now hearing about it? Somebody knocked out Gerald and stole some drugs. He's got a concussion but they say he's gonna be all right." He started to launch into his usual discourse about drugs and the state of mankind, but, remembering Mitch's absence, asked, "What's up with the trip to Nashville? What was that all about?"

Mitch just shook his head and walked back to find Sheriff Duggan.

This time the office was empty. Mitch decided to leave him a note and walked around the desk to get a pen and notepad. He stopped in his tracks, his eyes on the trashcan protruding from under the desk. He reached down and pulled out the fat brown envelope, still sealed. He turned it over in his hands, thinking about the last 24 hours: the directions to nowhere, the sheriff not taking his calls, the odd encounter with "Pony-tail" at the Parthenon, the run-around at Vanderbilt, and now the evidence package thrown away, unopened. Without hesitation he ripped it open, almost certain of what he would find. After flipping through the contents, he angrily threw the envelope and papers back into the trash can. The can teetered on its side before turning over, spilling the blank sheets of copy paper onto the floor.

***

With shaky hands, Sara put the car in reverse and backed out of the parking space. "He was busy. I'll take you back home."

Jessie gave an exasperated sigh. "I may be old but I'm not blind. I saw him, too...It may not be what you think."

"Yeah, maybe. I'm just not sure I want to find out right now. I'll talk to him later, okay?"

Jessie nodded, wondering if what they'd seen was exactly what it appeared to be. She knew that Mitch and Ali had dated off and on for years; Sara and Mitch had known each other less than a week. Expecting tears at any second, Jessie was surprised to see the girl's features relax. As she watched, she saw a calmness she hadn't seen before.

Feeling her gaze, Sara turned to her and forced a smile. "You know, I think it's going to be okay. But if it's not, I think I can deal with it." She paused, choosing her words. "When I saw him with that girl, I started to get mad, and then I heard my mother—and you—saying 'kiss it up to God.' I'm not saying if it's meant to be it's meant to be. I like Mitch a lot, and I know he likes me. I want love and faith and trust in my life, and I'm beginning to realize that if I want those things, I have to be willing to give them."

They drove for a couple of minutes in silence, each absorbed in their own thoughts. Suddenly, Jessie noticed the direction Sara was driving. "Oops. You turned the wrong way. Take a left at the stop sign, then go right, then go a little ways and take another right. That will get us back to my street."

A minute later Sara slowed the car. Their circuitous route had taken them by the hospice. Half a dozen people were gathered on the lawn, talking and glancing nervously at the building. "Look," Sara said, "isn't that Karen?"

They pulled over as Jessie rolled down her window. "Karen, what's going on?"

Karen saw Jessie's car and walked to the curb. "Hi. You haven't heard, have you?" At their blank stares, she explained, "Somebody attacked Gerald, then broke into the drug cabinet. Alice called and asked me to come back and help out while things were cleaned up."

"Is Gerald all right?"

"Yes, he's fine. Alice put him in the empty room, and you can believe he didn't like that one bit. He was hit from behind, so he didn't see who it was. It happened after we left." She rolled her eyes. "I'm sorry, that's obvious, isn't it? I guess I'm still flustered. And surprised. You'd think if someone were going to steal something, they'd come at night when the fewest number of people are on the floor, not during lunch, one of the busiest times. I don't understand it. We've never had problems like this before."

Stunned, Jessie stared at her friend as a sinking feeling washed over her.

"What is it, Jessie? Are you all right? You look like you're going to be sick."

"Oh, no. Oh, no." She clutched her hands over her chest and looked at her friend with a pained expression. "I think I've done something terrible."

Frank was pacing on the porch when the women pulled into the driveway. They were barely out of the car when Mitch drove in behind them and sprung from his car. Simultaneously, the men began talking but stopped mid-sentence when they saw Sara rush around to the passenger side to help Jessie out.

In seconds, Mitch was at her side and together they walked Jessie up the steps and into the living room, gently easing her onto the couch.

"What happened?" Frank asked, leaning over her and taking her hand. "Do you need a doctor?"

"I...I'll be fine. Sara, would you get me a glass of water?" Watching her go into the kitchen, she turned to Mitch. "You know about the attack at the hospice? I think it's my fault."

"What attack?" Frank interrupted impatiently. "Will somebody tell me what happened?"

"I don't know much. I was on my way back from Nashville when it happened—or maybe I was here with you, I'm not sure. And Jessie, it's not your fault. If you'd been there, you couldn't have stopped it." Mitch told them the few details he knew, glancing at Sara while he talked, trying to read her mood. "But that's not why I came over." He paused, looking at Frank. "Something odd is going on."

"Of course something odd is going on. It's been odd around here all week." Frank pulled the newspaper clipping from his shirt pocket and waved it in front of them.

"There's more." Mitch quickly told them about the pony-tailed stranger that he'd seen first at the gallery and then in Nashville. "I'm positive he knew who I was, but we'd never met. And then the package I was sent all over Nashville for was nothing. The sheriff threw it away without even opening it." He hesitated. "I hate to say it, but I'm afraid the sheriff is somehow involved."

Jessie interrupted. "That's impossible. Dave's nothing like those men at the art gallery." Her color had returned and she seemed herself again. "And the robbery? I wasn't saying I thought I could have stopped it. That's absurd. What I meant was just what I said: IT WAS MY FAULT."

Now that she had their attention, she explained. "Last night at the gallery, that skinny little man was asking me all about the hospice. That was after I said I couldn't go to the gallery this morning because of my volunteer job. He asked me so many questions and he looked so poorly himself I thought he might be sick, like with AIDS. I know that's prejudiced of me, but that's what I thought. Anyway, he seemed so, well, desperate for information, and specifically about medications, and asked were patients kept pain-free, and how many doctors and nurses worked there. You remember, Francis, I talked to him for a long time. You had to stop me because it was late and time to go. I think it was him. I think he did it."

When no one objected to her theory, she put her head in her hands. "Poor Gerald. I'll never be able to face him again."

The front door screen slammed as Karen came into the room. "I heard the last part. Jessie, do you really think it was him?" She sat down beside her. "Alice said the morphine was gone. Nothing else was taken. She's pretty upset, but most of the patients don't know that anything happened. We had to tell the family members who were either in the building or who saw the squad cars outside, but as far as I know, everyone is calmed down and things are nearly back to normal. Has something else happened? You all look upset."

Mitch elected not to repeat his story of the stranger and the phony evidence. "Frank, you started to say something earlier. Did you learn anything?"

Frank nodded grimly. "I believe so," he said, telling them his conjecture about the phone number. "But I don't want to call just yet. What we need is to get their phone numbers and see if one matches. Then if it matches, we've got to notify the authorities—the sheriff's office or something bigger. I think these guys have stolen something extremely valuable."

The others looked puzzled and began questioning him. He just shook his head and said, "Not yet."

Slapping his head, Mitch said, "I've got a number. Remember, Sara, when we were there the first time? The owner wrote his cell number on a piece of paper and gave it to me." He grimaced. "I was supposed to give to you, Jessie, but I forgot. I must have put it in my pocket." He mechanically checked all his pockets.

"What were you wearing?" Karen asked.

"Cutoffs." Sara answered for him. "You were wearing a white polo shirt and blue-jean cutoffs. You folded the piece of paper and put it in your right pocket."

Mitch looked curiously at her. "What?" she said, shrugging. "I just remembered, that's all."

Karen stood. "You all stay here. I'll run home and find it and call you with the number. If it matches, you have to call the sheriff. We can't wait any longer, not after what happened today."

***

Burton glanced up when the bell chimed, and his heart skipped a beat at the sight of a uniformed man approaching.

"Burton Roberts? I'm Sheriff Dave Duggan. Is your partner here?"

"Harris? I don't know where he is. What's wrong, officer?"

"There's been an assault and robbery. Your friend was implicated. Where is he?"

"Assault and robbery? Harris? That's impossible."

"Where is he?" His hand moved over his holster.

"I don't know. He was gone when I got up this morning."

The sheriff stood silently, waiting. It was a tactic that often worked for him. The other person would get nervous and start talking to fill the silence, usually saying more than they intended. This time though, the quiet was broken by the ringing of the sheriff's own cell phone. He inwardly cursed while he pulled it from his pocket and abruptly walked out of the shop to the sidewalk. Two minutes later he returned, a grim look on his face. "What kind of a car does he drive?"

"Excuse me?"

"What kind of a car does your partner drive?"

"A silver Cherokee. And it's my car. It's gone, too. I assume he's driving it."

"Not anymore. A silver Jeep was totaled today on I-40, west of here, and the driver fits your man's description. He was unconscious. And the trooper said he was carrying enough pain killers to put down an elephant."

Burton swallowed hard, quickly absorbing the implications. *Everything changes now*, he thought. He tried to look concerned. "He was unconscious when they found him? Is he going to make it?"

"Don't know."

"Where did they take him?"

"Probably Crossville. But ultimately he'll be back here, as a guest in my jail. It appears your man knocked out a nurse's aide at the hospice down the street and stole drugs. He stole medicine from dying people." Shaking his head with disgust, the sheriff slipped his phone back into his pocket. He looked around. "Looks like you're on your own here."

After the sheriff left, Burton went to the door and turned the Open sign around to Closed. Before he could turn the deadbolt, the door pushed open.

"Trouble with the law?"

Startled, he backed away from the big man with the odd gray pony-tail. "No, no, nothing important. I didn't expect you today."

The man removed his sunglasses. "I talked to my client and he's authorized me to meet your price. But it's got to happen now. Meet me in an hour at the crossroads just outside of town, by that boarded-up beer joint. Know the place?"

Burton nodded. "But one hour doesn't give me much time. I-I don't have a car."

The man's gaze turned icy. "That's your problem. Just don't be jerking me around. I've done my part. Now you'd better come through." He turned and walked away.

***

A half hour had passed since Karen left. Sara fussed over Jessie. Frank paced, going from the living room to the dining room and back. Mitch went from the living room to the porch and back, looked out windows, checked his watch, and avoided Sara's face. He wanted to ask her about the bags sitting in the living room, but he didn't.

Frank broke first. "Call her."

The younger man's phone was already in his hand, hitting the speed dial. No answer. "Something must have happened. She would have called by now. I'm going over there. Frank, I'll call your phone in five minutes."

Five minutes passed, then five more. Frank picked up the wrinkled newspaper ad. "This is ridiculous," he said, picking up his phone. "I'm calling the number. If Burton Roberts answers, we'll know. If he doesn't, then, well, we'll know that, too, won't we?" He punched in the numbers.

"Hello?" It was Burton.

"Mr. Roberts? This is Frank Cunningham. Jessie's young neighbor gave us this number to call you." He took a deep breath to calm his nerves. "She'd like to bring the paintings over. Is now a good time?"

After hanging up, he put the phone and newspaper ad on the end table, and gave urgent instructions to the women. "Sara, quick, find a sheet or blanket. We'll wrap up one of the paintings and I'll take it to him. I'll tell him you and Jessie are bringing over the other two. As soon as I leave here, Jessie, I want you to call the sheriff and tell him we think there is some very valuable stolen art at the gallery, and that the owner may be about to skip town. Tell him we have proof. Sara, stay here with Jessie and lock the doors. I'll leave my phone here in case Mitch calls."

"What are you going to do?" Jessie asked.

"Stall him, that's all. If his partner did the robbery, then this Mr. Roberts, or whatever his real name is, isn't going to stick around."

Sara brought a small lap quilt from her bedroom and spread it open on the coffee table. Frank gently took down one of the three Chagall-like paintings and together they folded the quilt around it. Jessie found a ball of twine in the kitchen and cut off enough to tie around their package. When they finished, Jessie led them into the living room, followed by Sara with the painting and Frank leaning heavily on his cane. When Jessie suddenly stopped, it nearly caused them all to collide.

Standing just inside the front door was Burton Roberts.

"I didn't mean to startle you," the intruder said. "The door was open. I hope you don't mind my coming in." He was wearing a sport coat and had a large canvas bag by his side.

Frank positioned himself in front of Jessie. Instinctively, he straightened to stand a little taller, knowing even as he did so that his posture of bravado was ill suited. He hadn't been in a fight in more than sixty years—and he'd lost that one. "You didn't have to walk over. We were just about to leave."

Burton eyed the quilted package and abruptly took it from Sara. "I'll save you the trouble. Tell me again, Mr. Cunningham, where did you say you got the phone number you used to call me? You said from a neighbor?"

Frank felt fear flow through his body, and he understood the expression of one's blood running cold. Calling that phone number had been a huge mistake.

"You see," Burton continued, casually leaning his bag and the quilt-wrapped painting against the wall by the door, "I have two phones." As he slipped his right hand into his jacket pocket, he looked behind Frank to Sara. "The number I gave you and your boyfriend wasn't the one you..." he looked back at Frank "used to call me. So where did you get the other number?"

Frank glanced out the front window. Where was Mitch? He prayed for the sound of sirens, or heavy steps and shouts bursting into the room. But there was only silence.

Feigning ignorance, he said, "I guess I was mistaken. I must have gotten the number from your partner." For a split-second, he thought the lie would work. Then his cell phone rang from the end table, inches from Burton, and all eyes turned to it. There, lying next to the phone, in plain sight, was the crinkled newspaper ad.

"What the hell?" Burton picked up the scrap of newsprint, looking quickly from the ad to Frank. Unanswered, the phone stopped ringing. "Who *are* you? Never mind. It doesn't matter." He glanced at his watch. Ten minutes left. "I don't have time to swap stories with you. It seems my partner had an 'incident' and left town in my car. But he left this behind." He pulled a small Smith & Wesson revolver from his pocket and pointed it at them. "It wasn't supposed to turn out like this." He sighed, his regret real. There had been moments when he had fantasized about another life, himself a legitimate, small-town businessman, possibly with a certain real estate lady by his side. But that wasn't going to happen. His voice turned cold. "I need a car. Give me your keys."

With a trembling voice, Jessie spoke. "The keys are in my purse. Please, just take the car and leave us alone."

A flick of motion caught Frank's eye. It was that damn cat, sitting on the back of the sofa, swishing her tail and staring at the other end of the couch. Why couldn't Jessie have a German shepherd instead? Or a Doberman?

Burton was scanning the room for Jessie's purse. Frank knew he only had a few seconds to act. "No, take mine. People around here would recognize her car. They won't notice you driving mine." He saw Sara turn to him and gave her a silencing look. He patted both pockets, as if searching for keys. "Oh, I forgot, I left my keys on the couch, over there, under that old hat."

Burton moved his gun to his left hand and with his right hand reached over to move the ratty straw hat, cautiously not taking his eyes or gun off the three people.

What happened next was nothing short of spectacular. Perhaps she sensed her mistress was in danger (Jessie's explanation). Perhaps she was reclaiming her earlier "kill" (Sara's theory). Or maybe it was just her mean streak (Frank's belief). In a split second, Gracie pounced and clamped onto his wrist, sinking her teeth into soft flesh while clawing furiously at his hand. As Burton yelled and turned to try to extract himself, Frank raised his cane and swung it down hard on the man's left arm. The gun fell and skidded across the room, and Sara went flying after it. Burton turned after her, tripping her with one hand while swinging his right arm to free himself of Gracie. Frank continued swinging his cane, connecting at least twice with Burton's head and once with a luckless lamp. Jessie aimed lower, grabbing onto one leg to keep him away from Sara. Sprawled on the floor, Sara reached the gun and slid it down the hallway out of sight. Gracie partially yielded to the flailing and unclenched her teeth—but not her claws—and added a horrific howl to the melee.

At some point they heard shouts and recognized the voices of Mitch and Sherriff Duggan. As quickly as it started, it was over.

The sheriff slapped handcuffs on Burton and hauled him out the door and onto the porch. "Jake Burton, you're being charged with theft, fraud, assault, breaking and entering, and whatever else I can come up with in the next 24 hours." He motioned for a deputy to take him. "Read him his rights and take him in. Oh, here, take this," he said, pulling a handkerchief from his back pocket and pointing to the man's handcuffed and bleeding hand. "Don't let him bleed all over the car."

Back in the living room, he surveyed the group. "Are you all okay? It's kind of hard to tell who was being rescued here." Leading Jessie to the sofa, he said, "Tell me what just happened. You can skip the earlier parts. Mitch filled me in on the way here."

Kneeling beside Sara, Mitch said, "The sheriff got to our house while Mom was looking for the phone number. She told him part of what had happened. Then I walked in and, well, after the Nashville trip, I wasn't sure who to trust. It took him a few minutes to explain." He looked painfully at Sara. "I should have known better. You all could have been hurt."

The sheriff grinned. "A little skepticism is good for the job. But—any later and you all would have had Burton in the hospital."

Jessie was beaming. "You should have seen these two," she said. They were both so brave."

Sitting next to her, Frank described the last hour, all the while patting her hand and watching Mitch fuss over Sara. Still on the floor, Sara was sitting up and had both hands around her ankle.

Out of nowhere, the pony-tailed stranger appeared and carefully picked up Burton's canvas bag.

"Well?" asked Sherriff Duggan. "Are they in there?"

Without looking at the others, the stranger said, "Dave, let's open this at your office." He looked at the package wrapped in the quilt. "What's that?"

"That's one of my husband's paintings. Mr. Burton said he wanted to hang it in his gallery, but I think he just wanted it for himself."

"May I see it?" the stranger asked.

Frank interrupted. "Who are you?"

"Sorry, folks," the sheriff said. "I should have introduced you. This is Peter McNiff. He's with the FBI's art crimes unit." He shrugged. "He's also my brother-in-law. He's been investigating the theft of some pretty valuable artwork that disappeared during Katrina, and he's been after Burton for a long time. *And*, he and I both have been keeping an eye on all of you. We thought you were going to spoil our trap."

As Frank, Jessie, and Sara stared at the law officers, they began to understand the danger they had escaped.

"May I see it?" the man repeated, nodding toward the wrapped up painting.

"Of course," Jessie answered, getting up. She gently untied and unwrapped the painting and held it up.

Peter McNiff gave a low whistle.

Pointing at the canvas bag, Frank said, "He had a real Chagall in there, didn't he?" The federal agent didn't have to answer; his astonishment told him he was right.

"Two. How did you know?"

"It was the ad. Once I figured out the phone number, I looked for letter combinations that would hold a hidden message. The ad said to contact Charles Gallager in Deer Creek. Charles—C-H-A. Gallager—G-A-L-L: *Chagall in Deer Creek.*

10. SATURDAY NIGHT

As promised, Sheriff Duggan and Agent McNiff returned to Jessie's after questioning Burton and finishing their paperwork. It had been a long day for all of them. Jake Burton was in jail. Matt Harris would join him soon.

After disappearing into the kitchen for a few minutes, Mitch and Agent McNiff returned to the crowded dining room with two kitchen chairs. Pillows propped up Sara's wrapped ankle. The little gallery had never had such an audience.

"Dave was telling us that the Chagall lithographs were stolen during Katrina," Frank said.

The FBI agent nodded, angling his chair to face Karen. "Most people don't know that millions of dollars of art were lost in Katrina, just in Mississippi alone," he explained. "Most of that was buried under sand and mud, or ripped to shreds by the storm, or destroyed in the waters. Pass Christian, Biloxi, Long Beach—all were hit hard. Believe it or not, there were reports of Picassos, a Rembrandt, and a da Vinci being lost."

Protesting, Karen said, "I just can't believe people would walk away and leave such valuables behind."

"You know what they say," he replied. "Hindsight is 20-20. No one believed it would be as bad as it was. Most people boarded up their homes and evacuated. Some moved valuables to an upper level, thinking if the storm was real bad, the most they'd get was flooding on the lower level. Who knew? Besides, some of those collections were so large, people couldn't carry them all. And, of course, some people weren't there; they were at their other homes, or traveling. Anyway, since then our office has been searching for pieces believed to have been stolen in the looting. One collector lost $2.6 million worth of artwork when his house was broken into."

As they listened intently, Gracie strutted through the room, stopping once to rub her face against the side of a chair. Maybe it was his imagination, but Frank thought she gave him a superior glare.

"When Jake Burton—your Burton Roberts—didn't go back to his job afterwards, his employer told his insurance company that he suspected the guy might have been responsible for taking pieces from his shop. The reason he suspected him was that he later heard from a couple of clients that they had been burglarized also. The icing on the cake was that both in the shop and in the clients' homes, the thief had been selective about what he took. He wasn't guessing. He knew what was valuable. Or, as we know now, Burton and his old friend Harris knew what was valuable."

Frank shook his head, puzzled. "I don't understand. How did they think they could sell famous artwork? Surely the stolen pieces would have shown up on some kind of list at an auction or a gallery? And why the newspaper ad? What was that all about?"

"Well, as you might guess, some art buyers aren't in it for art's sake, but just for the money. They know the thief can't sell a piece for its real value, so they get it for a reasonable price and then resell it to some mega-rich collector who has more money than some countries, and fewer scruples. These middle-man buyers can be organized crime, drug cartels, or even supporters of terrorist groups. They all use the profits to finance their organizations.

"As for the ad, at first glance it seems like a lame scheme, but that was also its attraction. With so many people believing the government spies on their cell phones, emails, and web sites, these guys thought they were outsmarting us by going old-school. They might have gotten away with it, too, except that we'd been tipped off to it by a source in Los Angeles." He paused, flashing a smile to Karen. "Sorry, I didn't mean to give you a dissertation. I don't usually have such a willing audience."

Jessie sighed. "Lordy, I am so relieved this is all over. What will happen to those men?"

"Although our sting got interrupted," Dave said, "since the stolen lithographs were in his possession, we have enough evidence to charge and convict Burton. And Harris has confessed and wants to work a deal. We think he'll turn on Burton."

"What about the art in their shop?" asked Karen. "Was it all stolen, too?"

"Three or four were," said the agent. "The rest were forgeries of other stolen pieces. Harris was an artist himself—and a remarkable forger. After Harris copied them, he and Burton sold the originals, then they'd sell the forgeries. So they were selling each piece twice. Since the artists of the stolen paintings were not widely known, these two guys were able to stay under our radar for a while."

Frank shook his head. "Wasted talent. Wasted lives."

"Yep, you're so right. Well, I'd better be going. It was a real pleasure meeting you all." He grinned conspiratorially at Mitch and turned to Karen. "Umm, your son mentioned to me earlier that he might be tied up here for a while. Do you by chance need a lift home?"

Blushing, she glanced at her son. "I'd like that."

"I'd best be getting home, too," the sheriff added. "Oh, by the way, Frank, drop by the gallery tomorrow morning and you can pick up those wooden boxes that belong to your friend. There's no need in tying them up in evidence."

The agent turned to Frank. "Those are yours? I saw them the other night. They're quite intriguing. I know a gallery owner—a legitimate one—who might be interested in selling them. I'd be glad to take them to him, if you'd like. He's always looking for new artists."

Frank couldn't have been happier.

For the next hour, the four rehashed the week's events, often shuddering at what could have been. The young couple held hands and all four refrained from talking of tomorrow and goodbyes.

When a cell phone beeped to announce a text message, Sara laughed. "Frank, you get more phone calls and texts than anyone I know. You must have a gazillion friends."

"It's not my phone this time. I think it's yours."

Warily, she walked across the room and retrieved it from her bag. Mitch winced, thinking it might be from the ex-boyfriend. Aloud, she read her father's text: "Plans changed. Will be home Sunday PM."

11. SUNDAY

"Oh, Frank, you can't do this. You can't afford..." Sara stopped abruptly and tried to back track. "I have the money Jessie paid me."

Eyebrows rose all around, both in curiosity and embarrassment for their old friend.

Suppressing his amusement, Frank assured her he could indeed afford the airline ticket. "In fact," he said, turning to Mitch, "if you care to join Sara, your mother and I are sending you on a well-deserved vacation." He gestured to the envelope in Sara's hand. "There are two boarding passes in there. Mitch, if you drive Sara to Knoxville, you can both catch a flight to Savannah, and Sara will be home when her dad gets there tonight."

Pointing to a carry-on on the sidewalk, Karen added, "I took the liberty."

Conflicted, the uniformed deputy made a weak protest. "But my shift starts in a couple of hours."

"Nope. Dave felt bad about sending you on a wild-goose-chase to Nashville, so he arranged a few days off for you."

Mitch grinned broadly, and turned to Sara. "I'm ready if you are."

Sara awkwardly limped to Frank and hugged him tightly. "Thank you," she said and, in a near whisper, added, "Thank you for everything. Thank you for rescuing me." When she pulled away, she brushed away a tear and said, "It's so hard to leave. Can I come back and visit all of you?"

Jessie held back her own tears. "There's always a room for you here."

After a flurry of more hugs and promises to stay in touch, the young couple drove off. Karen sighed heavily and grabbed Jessie's hand. "I know he'll be back in a few days, but it's never going to be the same again, is it? He's in love." Her eyes brimmed with tears and she laughed at herself. "And look at me—I'm crying over him and I'm about to jump in the fire myself."

***

After paying the taxi driver, Mitch unloaded their bags and helped Sara out of the cab. Seeing the lights on in her house, she discreetly kissed her fingertips and flicked her fingers upwards.

Inside the house, a travel-weary professor sat glumly, Sara's note in his hand. Hearing car doors slam, he rose and looked out the window and saw his wayward daughter with a policeman gripping her arm. Alarmed and incensed, he went outside to see how bad the trouble was.

But instead of guilt or shame, his daughter's face was one of radiance. As she stepped toward him, he saw the bandaged ankle and an old-fashioned walking cane, and his anger was instantly replaced with fatherly concern. Awkwardly, he reached for her and was shocked when she flung herself into his arms.

"Dad! I didn't think you'd be home yet. How was your trip? I've got so much to tell you—I guess you've already read that awful note I left you. I'm so sorry. I've been such a brat. But that's all over. I'll tell you all about it later. But first, I want you to meet someone very, very special."

Before introducing the beaming young man by her side, she hugged her stunned father again, thinking how good it felt to trust in love.

***

While Jessie puttered around in the kitchen, Frank checked on Bill and gave him the short version of the weekend's events, leaving out the part about the gun and any danger the group might have faced.

"How about you? When can you go home?"

"I'm home now. They released me yesterday. I had to promise to change my diet and—you'll be glad to know—my attitude. Thanks, buddy."

"For what?"

"For saving me from myself."

"Just get well and get back to the diner."

"I can't wait. I have to tell you, that guy you found for us is a genius. The first day, I was annoyed when Mary told me that customers were raving over his cooking. They actually stand at the counter to watch him cook. I have to admit, I like his cooking, too. Mary brought samples to the hospital so I could taste for myself. I don't know where you found him, but he's great. I have this idea—tell me what you think. If we can sustain the customer count, maybe we can keep him on permanently and revamp the menu. I wouldn't want to totally change it, just tweak it some. Less frying, fresher, healthier. Still basic diner food, but different. It could be just what we've been needing."

After a promise to stop by tomorrow, Frank hung up. *So*, he thought, *Bill and Sara think I do rescue missions and Jessie thinks I try to change people. Is that what I've become, a silly self-appointed savior to the people around me?*

In the kitchen, Jessie used a plastic card to scrape off the last bits of fried chicken that were stuck on her skillet. Finally satisfied, she rinsed the heavy iron skillet and carefully set it on the stove to dry. She gently wiped off the card, smiling sadly at the face of her old friend Geraldine. She'd miss the old lady who had so cheerfully shared her quirky housekeeping tips with her through the years. How hard it must have been for her the morning she handed Jessie her driver's license. She quickly tucked it into the drawer and went to the living room. She found Frank staring out the front window, frowning.

"Quarter for your thoughts."

"Oh, just wondering." He suddenly smiled. "Look, the lightning bugs are out. Want to sit on the porch?" He put down his phone and led her to the glider. He missed the cane, but he'd get used to it.

They sat quietly, the glider squeaking, as they watched dozens of lightning bugs flash their golden beacons at one another. Jessie made a funny noise.

"Jessie, did you just giggle?"

She chuckled. "I was just thinking. People aren't so evolved, are they?"

"How so?"

"These little bugs fly around, blinking their lights to attract one another. And Mitch and Sara and Karen and that FBI man—they may as well have been wearing flashing neon signs saying 'choose me, choose me!'"

They laughed together, enjoying the moment, then grew serious again.

"While you were on the phone, I called Alice to check on Gerald. He's fine now, but she told me I'm off the schedule for the whole week. She said I needed the break. And Karen's packing for Nashville, so I won't see her for a while. It's going to be a quiet week. I wish you didn't have to go back tomorrow."

"Yes, me, too." He sighed. "But those men are locked up now, and you're safe. And I need to check on Bill, and I've got..."

"I know, I know. It's like Sara said last night. You have a 'gazillion' friends." She looked at him curiously. "Just what is it that you do, Francis?" she asked. "I've often wondered why you were always so busy, but I didn't want to pry."

Avoiding her eyes, he said, "What do you mean?"

"Never mind. It's none of my business." She sounded hurt, and that hurt him.

Turning to face her, he took her hand—and a leap of faith. "I do some investing," he said. "Emmie and I did it together, and after she died, I just kept on."

"You play the stock market?"

"No. I invest in people."

Confused, she asked, "How do you do that?"

"There's this company called Shellott. It provides the money for, uh, situations. Rent, school, wages, whatever is needed by the person who's being funded. In turn, each person has to commit to do something for someone else. But it's not one of those 'pay it forward' projects where someone does a good deed indiscriminately for a stranger—who may not really need the help or even appreciate it. And there's no deadline for the pay-back. In fact, that's part of the plan, that each person carry a commitment in his head for a lifetime, waiting for the moment where his help will be meaningful. It's designed to promote a lifetime of compassion and prudence and hard work."

Jessie looked at him quizzically. "Shalott? Like The Lady of Shalott?"

"No, S-h-e-l-l-o-t-t."

"Oh. So, you work for this Shellott company?"

"Not exactly." He gripped her hand, nervous about her response. "I am the company."

"I don't understand. Anthony never mentioned...Emmie never said..."

"Tony didn't know. The kids don't even know. Emmie didn't want anyone to know—especially the children. She was so afraid the money would corrupt their lives. The plan was to spend it to help out a few people who were down on their luck, then it would be gone and we'd just live out our retirement on our pensions and Social Security. We had enough, and we thought, at our age, we just didn't need more." He shrugged. "But it didn't turn out that way. We hired someone to handle the money for us, and, it just kept growing. Now spending it, or managing it, has become a full-time job."

She stared at him, dumbfounded. "That young man Jose who came by today and put a battery in your car?" He nodded. "The wing at the hospice?" He nodded again. She narrowed her eyes. "The money to fix up my house?" Another nod.

"But the money for you wasn't charity. It was a gift." He sighed. "So now you know, and I suppose you were right. I do try to change people, and I do meddle in their lives." He searched her face, wanting answers to his own questions. "Do you think that's egotistic, to want to redirect people's lives?"

"Oh, Francis, I never thought that. I've always thought you were kind and generous. How could what you're doing be anything but good? Whether the money helps someone at a fork in the road or at the end of the road, it's all good."

He sighed again. He wanted her understanding, not just pat answers. "Emmie and I wanted to do something significant. Although sometimes I think it's just spitting in the ocean...how can one person or one action make a difference in the grand scheme of things?"

She thought that over for a minute, then patted his hand with affection. "Whether it's an act of kindness or, in their case," she nodded toward the gallery, "an act of greed, it all makes a difference. Maybe each bit of goodness offsets the evil and keeps balance in this world. Lord knows what would happen if we didn't try."

They grew silent again, until she could contain it no longer. "But where did the money come from?"

He hesitated. "This is Emmie's secret, okay?" She pulled back her hand and, like a girl sixty years younger, made an X across her heart. "Remember how excited Emmie was when Tennessee got the lottery? Every week, when we filled up at the Shell station, she'd go inside and buy a ticket."

Her eyes widened. "Ohhh, now I get it. *Shellott.*"

She laughed, and he began to tell her the stories, some sad, some happy. The more he talked, the more relaxed they both were. For a little while it was like old times, and they felt the presence of their lost loves. They talked about them, too, but this time it was less about loss and more about how full their lives had been and still were.

They laughed, talked some more, and laughed again, rocking the glider while the lightning bugs flickered around them.

ACKNOWLEDGEMENTS

This man walks into a restaurant... Have you ever seen a stranger and wondered what his story was? Well, that's how this book was born, over lunch with two extraordinary friends who saw the spark and fanned the flame. Thank you Jeri Parker and Jamie Smith for being there, literally and figuratively, every step of the way.

Thanks also Jamie for your invaluable advice from your experience as a hospice volunteer coordinator. Likewise, thank you Harriet Calandros for providing your expertise as a hospice nurse. The caring attention of hospice staff and volunteers for those in their last days is simply extraordinary and inspiring.

Agreeing to read the initial draft for a first-time author is a leap of faith. For taking that leap, thank you Jeri, Jamie, Harriett, Helen Harwood, Annell Gerson, Linda Purnell, Susan Jones, and Sue Wilson. I so much appreciate the hours you spent, your candid advice, your thoughtful encouragement.

Publishing a first book is a daunting experience. To Bob Babcock, Ashley Clarke, Jan Babcock, and Mark Babcock—the team at Deeds Publishing—I cannot thank you enough for your support and diligent efforts. Hand-holding a rookie author must require incredible patience; I appreciate yours more than you know.

Last, but always first, thank you David and Kate, for your encouragement throughout this adventure—and more importantly, for bringing love and joy to my life. No one could ever write better characters for a husband and daughter than you have been to me.

ABOUT THE AUTHOR

Artful Deception is Peggy Spear's first novel. After a career of professional writing for daily newspapers, a major university, and the private sector, she turned her hand to fiction, creating characters drawn from a lifetime's observations. A practicing skeptic but wannabe Pollyanna, Peggy believes in the magic of books, the comfort of friends, the goodness of kindness, the wisdom of cats, the honor of integrity, the genius of Van Gogh, and the healing properties of a warm Krispy Kreme donut. An amateur artist as well, she reads, writes, paints, and lives in Roswell, GA.

DISCUSSION QUESTIONS

1. Frank uses his resources to help needy people better their lives and to instill in them a commitment to do the same for others down the road. How does this differ from "pay it forward" and "acts of random kindness" celebrated in the media?

2. Jessie explains to Sara that the hospice is a refuge for patients at life's end. In what other ways is "refuge" a recurring theme in this book?

3. Artful Deception is categorized as a cozy mystery, but there's no murder. Would this book have been more interesting with a murder (or sex scenes or profanity)? Discuss the significance of violence in entertainment today. Do you think readers would want books to be rated like movies?

4. This book deals frequently with death: Frank's wife, Jessie's husband, Sara's mother, Mitch's father, and hospice patients. Did you find this depressing or sad? If not, why?

5. When Sara meets Jessie, she almost immediately drops her defiant/defensive demeanor. Did you think this behavior was out of character, or her true character? Why do you think she responded this way to Jessie but not to Frank?

6. Do you know anyone like Frank? Do you believe people that genuinely kind and generous actually exist? What did you think of Jessie's criticism that Frank tried to change people?

7. Do you identify with the world as Frank sees it? If you are a baby boomer, you maybe recall picking up hitchhikers or giving food to drifters passing through your neighborhood. Is Frank a product of his era? Could you be as trusting as Frank? Would you ever take a stranger into your home?

8. Did you grow up in a small town? Do you think the size of your town or community helped shape who you are today?

9. Abandoned by her boyfriend, Sara decides to find a way back home without calling family or friends. Instead, she turns to a stranger. Do you think she did this to avoid embarrassment or an "I told you so" response from her father or girlfriends, or do you think she did this to prove something to herself?

10. "Kiss it up to God" is a version of the five-second rule for eating food that's been dropped on the floor. When Sara heard Jessie say it, she broke down at a childhood memory of her mother using that phrase. How does Sara use the thought behind this expression to help her overcome distrust?

CPSIA information can be obtained
at www.ICGtesting.com
Printed in the USA
FFOW03n0348160417
34492FF

9 781944 19390